Stranded in a Small Town Christmas

holiday h•e•a

NEW YORK TIMES BESTSELLING AUTHOR

SHANNON STACEY

Will a billionaire stranded by a winter storm lose his heart to the small-town innkeeper willing to help him... for a price?

Natalie

When I gave my aunt a ride to the airport ten days before Christmas, I didn't expect to bring a stray billionaire back to Charming Lake. I agreed to give him a ride in exchange for one hundred thousand dollars—needed for reasons I don't share with him—but the weather took an icy turn and now I'm bringing him home with me.

Donovan

Thanks to losing my wallet and phone—and weather gone wrong—I'm stranded at The Charming Inn with a *very* distracting woman. I don't like distractions. Swept up in the town's Christmas celebrations, though, I can't keep my hands off of her. How can I be falling so hard and fast for a woman who put a six-figure price tag on helping me?

If you're in the mood for a festive read full of love, laughter and happily ever after, the HOLIDAY HEA series is here for you!

CHAPTER *One*

Natalie

OF COURSE, the day I finally meet a super hot billionaire in a killer suit, the only thing I feel is an overwhelming desire to punch him in the dick.

I can't stand rude people, and he's seriously dimming my holiday spirit.

It's already suffering. I'd do almost anything for my family—and they know it—which is why I'm currently navigating a previously undiscovered level of hell ten days before Christmas. And a winter storm is forecast to hit any minute, so that's a fun bonus.

The Manchester-Boston Regional Airport isn't *actually* hell, of course. It's really nice, to be honest. And it isn't previously undiscovered, either, considering how many people have bumped into me. I'd rather be almost anywhere else.

But it's my aunt's first holiday since losing her

husband (to another woman, but we don't talk about that) and my cousin bought Aunt Marilyn a plane ticket to Georgia so she can spend Christmas with her. Aunt Marilyn asked my mother for a ride to the airport, and since I drive a Jeep and my mom signs my paychecks, I got volunteered.

"At least she's not flying out of Logan, so you don't have to drive to Boston," my mom had said when I gave her the classic sigh-and-eye-roll combination daughters master well before adolescence and rarely outgrow.

Aunt Marilyn's through security and officially out of my hands, so it's time to caffeinate and get out before the picturesque flurries I arrived in turn treacherous. I've almost reached the tail end of the line for coffee when a raised male voice catches my attention.

Nearby, a tall man with dark hair in a sharp business suit is arguing with two airport employees. They look tired and he looks angry, and I frown. Jerks who take their anger out on people who don't deserve it is definitely near the top of my pet peeves list, along with people who don't like dogs and shoppers who put unwanted groceries back on the wrong shelves.

He's undeniably attractive—physically, at least—and I wander a little closer as I listen to the exchange. It sounds like he left something on the plane, and there's a procedure for dealing with that. I get the impression the employees have explained the procedure to him several times already, but apparently he thinks he's special.

"Why won't anybody help me?" he demands, not yelling exactly, but definitely with an aggressiveness in his tone.

"Maybe because you're being a jerk," I say loudly, unable to help myself. "But hey, there's still time for the

Ghost of Christmas Future to visit and show you the error of your ways so you can stop making everybody else's holiday stress worse because you can't keep track of your carry-on crap."

He turns to face me and I brace myself for a blast of the airport equivalent of road rage. At least he won't be unleashing it on people who can't dish it back to him without losing their jobs, though.

The man looks at me, his blue eyes so intense I shiver, and I wait for the yelling to start. Instead, he deflates slightly—there's no other word for the way his expression and tense body soften—and runs his hand over his hair. Judging by its messy state, it isn't the first time he's done it today.

Then he turns back to the employees he's been arguing with. "I'm sorry. I understand you've done what you can, and I apologize for taking my frustration out on you."

My eyebrows arch in surprise. That isn't the outcome I'd been expecting. And I'm even more shocked when he turns to face the people behind him, waiting for assistance, and apologizes to them for the unpleasant disruption before walking away.

When the man sits on a bench, I know that's my cue to move on. There's a long line for coffee and I want to hit the road. But when he props his elbows on his knees and drops his head into his hands, I can't bring myself to walk away. It isn't in my nature to ignore somebody who's obviously in distress, even if he made a horrible first impression. He *did* apologize, after all.

"You okay?" I ask, sitting on the bench next to him. He shakes his head without lifting it, and I have no idea what to say next.

Then he sits up straight so quickly it startles me, and he

waves a hand at the lines of people. "What good is being a billionaire if I can't get out of a damn airport?"

A *billionaire?* That's new. I've never met a billionaire before, but it explains his temper tantrum. The guy's probably used to getting his way. "Are you really?"

"Yeah." He turns those blue eyes on me again. "I can't prove it, though."

"What's your name?"

"Donovan Wilson."

"I'm Natalie. Natalie Byrne," I say to be polite while I type his name into Google. A few clicks later and I'm staring at a stern photo of him—not a dark hair out of place—on a website that talks about holdings and portfolios and stuff. "Okay, so just buy the airport and then they'll *have* to help you."

He snorts. "If I could prove who I am, I wouldn't need to buy the airport. I left my briefcase on the plane."

"Did you check the lost and found?" I ask, and he sighs. Of course he did. "Sometimes it takes a while for stuff to turn up."

"They said it could be hours, *if* it's found." He shakes his head. "I don't have hours. I have to get out of here *now.* I'd come back another day for the briefcase, but my phone and my wallet are in it, so I'm stuck in an airport with absolutely no way to call anybody or rent a car. Or buy the airport."

"You put your phone and your wallet in your briefcase?" I ask, belatedly realizing he probably isn't in the mood for that question.

Red tints his cheeks, and I'm not sure if it's anger or chagrin. "I left a meeting and went straight to the airport. I keep my wallet and my phone in my suit coat pocket, but I knew I'd get hot on the plane and take the coat off. I didn't want them to fall out, so I locked them in the briefcase, which the attendant made me put at my feet. I rarely carry the briefcase with me when I fly and I was so focused on getting off the plane, I left it."

"You must have an assistant or two—or twenty. You can use my phone to call one of them."

"Thanks, but there are two numbers I know off the top of my head. One of them isn't answering, and the other's on an island getting married and I told her to turn her phone off for the occasion because I didn't want to forget and call her."

"You'd forget she's getting married?" That sounds like something a billionaire would do.

"She's been my right hand for more than a decade. It's a habit to reach out when I need something—like when I find myself stranded in an airport with no money or identification."

I'm still clicking around his site. "Can't you contact people through the website? There are a lot of numbers and email addresses here."

"I don't employ the kind of people who would give my credit card number to anybody who calls the contact number claiming to be me," he snaps, his frustration coming through again.

"Okay, so call your credit card company. Or do you pay people to remember your mother's maiden name and the street you grew up on?" The look he gives me probably scares the crap out of people who care if he's mad at them. I'm not one of them, so I shrug. "Just a suggestion."

"I don't have time for that. I need to get to Stowe right now." His jaw flexes. "It's an emergency."

"Oh no. Did some fourth-generation small business owner refuse to sell his soul to you?"

I expect another of those potent glares, but he's too busy looking around as if somebody's going to swoop in and save him. People probably do that on a regular basis. "It's a family emergency. There's nothing in Vermont I want to buy."

"With your charm and holiday spirit, I'm sure people will line up to help you," I say, standing up because I'm about to walk away. I don't want to end up in a ditch because I was listening to a poor little rich guy's problems. I don't have any cash on me, so there's not much I can do for him. "Good luck."

"Wait. You're leaving, right? I'll pay you to drive me to Stowe."

I hesitate. "You already told me you have no money."

"No, I told you I have a *lot* of money. I just don't have it on me right now." He stands, practically vibrating with tension. "I can get you the money within days. Before Christmas, so you'll have time to buy more presents for people."

I ask myself if any amount of money is worth spending two and a half hours—or more, depending on the snow—trapped in a vehicle with this man.

I already know the answer to that, though. And I also know the amount. "I'll get you to Stowe. For one hundred thousand dollars."

CHAPTER *Two*

Donovan

HAVING ACCUMULATED MORE money than I ever dreamed possible has taught me that people will always want a piece of it. Nobody even bothers pretending they're going to pay for lunch anymore—not that I'd let them, but they could offer—and a former friend stopped speaking to me when I refused to buy him a second home in the Caribbean for his birthday. I don't like it, but I'm used to it.

Maybe that's why I can't explain the soul-deep pang of disappointment I feel when the beautiful woman with the prickly attitude puts a six-figure price tag on helping me.

She has a cloud of dark brown hair barely restrained in a very messy bun by one of those fluffy elastic things. It's red with a candy cane pattern, which matches the red sweater she's wearing with worn jeans that hug her curves. Her eyes are even darker than her hair, and her naked but rosy lips draw my eyes even when they're twisted into a wry smile.

Natalie Byrne would draw my eye anywhere we crossed paths. It's unfortunate it happens to be here—in an airport I can't leave without giving into her blatant extortion. *Merry Christmas,* I think with a sarcastic twist.

"Done," I say, because I'm out of options other than waiting around this airport for an undetermined amount of time.

Her eyes widen, and I try not to think about how beautifully dark they are. "Seriously? You'll give me one hundred thousand dollars if I drive you to Stowe?"

"Yes, seriously. Were *you* not serious?"

Natalie blinks and then gives a sharp nod. "Yes. I'm serious."

"Let's go, then." There's something else I desperately need, though, and I'm willing to swallow my pride to get it. "Any chance you'll buy me a coffee for the road?"

"Sure," she says easily. "I'll add it to your tab."

The line for coffee moves quickly, which is good because I don't know what to say and I'm stuck with awkward silence. Natalie's texting somebody and I can't see her screen, but I assume she's letting somebody know she's making a detour to Stowe, Vermont with a man she just met—along with my name and the link to my website.

During the walk to the short-term parking lot, I learn two things. One, the white stuff falling out of the sky is more of a wintery mix than snow. And two, the shoes I'd worn to sit in meetings all day aren't great in icy slush. I don't fall on my ass or spill my coffee, but I come close several times as I try to keep up with Natalie in her weather-appropriate boots.

Since I can't manage her pace without sacrificing my

caffeine or my dignity—or both—she already has her Jeep Wrangler running when I get there. She pulls a coat and gloves out of the backseat, along with a scraper.

"I'll do that," I say, because I'm not going to sit in the vehicle while she cleans the accumulated white crust off her windshield.

She laughs at me. "In those shoes? With no coat and gloves? If you die of hypothermia, I won't get my money, so get in and drink your coffee."

Short of physically wrestling her for possession of the scraper—which might have sounded appealing if we weren't in a frigid parking lot—all I can do is what I'm told. My toes and the hand not holding the coffee are already aching from the cold, so I slip into the passenger seat and try to convince myself I shouldn't feel guilty. I *am* paying a hundred grand for a two-and-a-half-hour ride, after all.

It doesn't work, though, and I'm about to get out and wrestle her for the scraper if I have to when her door opens and she tosses the scraper into the back as she slides into the seat.

"Buckle up, buttercup," she says as she fastens her seatbelt.

I've definitely never been called buttercup before, but she's already navigating her way toward the lot's exit and I keep my mouth shut until we're safely on the highway. Finally, I can't take it anymore.

"Can I borrow your phone to make a call?"

"Sure." Natalie pulls it out of one of those holders that jam into the heating vent, holds it up so her face can unlock it, and then hands it to me.

I use the keypad to punch in one of only two numbers I know by heart and listen to the ringing. So does Natalie, since the hands-free automatically routes the call through her Jeep's speakers. I hang up when I hear my mom's voice inviting me to leave her a message.

I want to call the ski resort, but I need to look up the number first. Using somebody's phone to make a call isn't the same as rummaging around in the apps, though. "Do you mind if I use the browser to search?"

She shrugs. "Go for it. Just don't search for anything that'll put me on a watch list."

A minute later, the Jeep is filled with the sound of a ringing phone again, but this time somebody answers, with Shea asking how she can help me.

"Hi Shea. My name is Donovan Wilson and my mother —Justine Wilson—is the guest who was injured on the slopes this morning. I flew into Manchester and I'm in route, but she's not answering her phone and I need to know which hospital she was taken to."

I'm aware of Natalie's head jerking toward me and I glance over to see her giving me a thoughtful look. It's a *long* look and she should be watching the road. I'm listening to Shea, though, so I just wave my hand at the windshield. Natalie rolls her eyes before turning them forward again.

When I have the information I need, I thank Shea and hang up the phone. That was the easy part. Getting information from the hospital is going to be harder, but maybe they can page my stepmother and get her on the phone.

"You could have said your mom's hurt and you're trying to get to her," Natalie says softly.

I'm searching on her phone again, looking for the hospital's number. "It would have taken even more time to explain and it doesn't change anything—I need to get to Stowe as soon as possible."

"Yeah, but you would have looked like less of a jerk."

I rarely care if people think I'm a jerk. One doesn't amass a fortune without stepping on toes, and though I've tried to build my company as ethically as possible, being liked isn't high on my priority list. It isn't on the list at all, actually.

But the way Natalie's voice softens—losing the snarky edge I've definitely deserved in the short time since we've met—makes my day feel brighter already, and I realize I might care if *she* likes me.

I need to focus on my mom, though, so I tap the number on the browser screen and confirm that I want to connect the call. Then I have to navigate through the directory menu until I'm finally connected to a person.

"This is Donovan Wilson. My mother, Justine Wilson, was brought in by ambulance following a ski accident and she's not answering her cell phone. I need to speak with somebody who can tell me what's going on." I think of Natalie sitting silently next to me. "Please."

"Hold, please."

I'm on hold for what feels like forever, and everything I've learned about self-control and projecting a solid, confidence-inspiring image has gone out the window. My knee is bouncing and I'm drumming my fingers on the lid of my coffee cup, waiting to hear if my mother is okay. Or if —god forbid—she isn't.

"Donovan!" My mother's voice booms through the Jeep's speakers, startling me for a moment. In the next second, I'm as close to crying as I ever remember being. "How are you, honey?"

"How am *I*? Mom. What happened? Are you okay?"

She laughs, and in my peripheral vision, I see Natalie cover her mouth, as if she's trying not to laugh along with my mom. "I sprained my ankle. It's bad, I guess, but nothing's broken. The medical team is wonderful here, and so are the hospital staff. They're taking very good care of me."

"I got a text message from Judy using your phone telling me you'd been in an accident and were being taken out in an ambulance, and then she never responded to my text or answered the many times I tried to call. I walked out of a meeting and got on the next plane out."

"A commercial flight?" She laughs again, and I hear Natalie snort. "You're not driving a rental car, are you? You hardly ever drive a car yourself, so you shouldn't be talking on the phone while you're behind the wheel."

"By some miracle, I was able to get the last seat on a commuter flight. And don't worry about me." I give Natalie the closest thing I have to a pleading look. "I have a driver."

Natalie not only rolls her eyes—she rolls her entire head. But she doesn't laugh in my face or say anything that will embarrass me.

"But back to you," I say to my mom. "Did you hit your head? Is there anything you're not telling me? I mean, Judy sounded panicked and then I couldn't reach her."

"You know Judy. I love the woman, but she gets distressed if I stub my toe. Staying calm while I'm being rescued from the side of a mountain isn't in her skill set. And she left her phone in our suite. I put mine in the outer pocket of my shell instead of inside and the cold killed the battery, so it died right after she sent you the text."

After hours of imagining the worst, listening to the teasing affection in Mom's voice as she talks about her wife releases the tension in my muscles. I lean my head back against the headrest with a sigh of relief.

"I'm just waiting for my discharge papers," she continues, "and then we're heading back to the resort. Judy said we'll order room service and watch movies."

I wince because crashing my mom and stepmom's anniversary trip isn't on my holiday to-do list. But there's no sense in going back to the airport until they find my briefcase. "I'll be there at—"

I glance at the phone, but there's no bubble at the top indicating the GPS is offering directions—and an ETA—in the background. When I look at her, Natalie shrugs and gestures at the swirling snow and flash of brake lights ahead of us. And a glance at her dashboard tells me we're doing thirty miles per hour under the highway's speed limit.

"I don't know when I'll get there, but I'm on my way. Can you see if they have a room for me at the resort? I don't care what kind of room, but I don't have my phone, so it's easier if you handle it when you get back."

"You don't have your phone?" Not only does she laugh, but I can hear Judy laughing in the background. "Not having your phone would require you to have actually set it down."

"It's a long story."

"Are you calling from your driver's phone, then? Can I reach you on it?"

I look over at Natalie again. She nods and then recites the number for my mother.

"I've got it," my mom says. "I hear the snow is really coming down, so be careful."

I'd just disconnected when Natalie mutters something and veers right unexpectedly, taking the exit we'd been about to pass by.

"Where are we going?"

She jerks her head back to the highway, where I can barely make out a mass of brake lights through the snow. And also some headlights, which means some of those stopped cars aren't facing the right direction. "The highway's going to be closed. We'll take the back roads."

The Jeep slides a little when Natalie reaches the stop sign at the bottom of the exit ramp, but I exhale when she brings it back in line.

Having control is important to me, but I have none, so all I can do is lean against the seat and try to relax. I don't know Natalie, but I can see she's a capable driver in the snow. Her vehicle has four-wheel drive.

My fate's in the hands of a pretty brunette I just met, who's singing "Last Christmas" off-tune under her breath. It'll be fine.

CHAPTER
Three

Natalie

I KNEW when I left home that, unless the meteorologist *really* got it wrong, I'd be driving home from the airport in the snow. No big deal. But this is definitely more of a wintry mix, and if it tips over into freezing rain, my Jeep and I are going to be in trouble.

And because no good deed ever goes unpunished, I'll be taking this guy along for the ride. It's not like I can abandon him somewhere with no phone and no wallet. Leave it to me to pick up a broke billionaire.

He smells good, though. A spicy scent that's too subtle to be cologne. Body wash, maybe. Or aftershave. And under that, a slight tang of sweat, probably from his stress in the airport. Donovan's scent blends nicely with the cranberry air freshener hanging from my radio knob, and my mouth waters a little. I'm hungry, and it's been a while since I've had a meal *or* a man. A billionaire wasn't necessarily to my taste, but he'd make a sweet snack.

It's probably a good thing keeping us on the road and facing the right direction keeps me from staring at him because I'm not sure I'd be able to stop. But the road's getting increasingly slippery and I keep having to consciously loosen my grip on the steering wheel when my fingers ache.

I picture the map of the storm I saw on the news, and I know it's going to be even worse when we cross over into Vermont and start heading north. If we make it that far, and it's a big if. Home, however, isn't that far away.

"Look," I finally say. "I know I promised I'd take you to Stowe and you want to get to your mom, but that was before the freezing rain came on the scene. I'm not sure I can get you there safely and, even if I could, it would probably be tomorrow before we get there."

"I agree," he says, and I can hear the tension in his voice. "So, what are the options?"

"Well, option one is you tell me you're not going to pay me because I didn't get you to Stowe, and I'll leave you in the next town. There's a gas station that'll probably still be open. I'll give you twenty bucks for food and a quarter for the pay phone."

"Do you still have working pay phones around here?"

"Actually, I don't think I've ever seen one in real life, so probably not."

"In that case, what's option two?"

"You promise you'll still pay me and I take you home with me." I don't take my eyes off the road, but it's impossible to miss the way his head whips around. "Okay, that sounded bad, but before you jump to any conclusions about my intentions, my family owns an inn and I run it for them. You can spend the night now that you know your mother's okay, and I can get you the rest of the way to Stowe as soon as the roads are clear."

"And you'll add the cost of the room to my tab?"

"Of course."

"Spending the night at an inn sounds more appealing than spending it in a gas station or a ditch—or worse—so I'll take option two."

Relief rushes through me, and I exhale slowly. While he's buckled into my passenger seat and therefore doesn't have a lot of say in where I drive, I'm thankful he's willing to roll with the change in plan.

Two miles later, I drop speed—not that I had much to start with—and take the slowest right turn ever onto the road that'll take me home. The state plows don't maintain it and it's been a while since a town truck has gone through. But there's less traffic on it and the accumulated crusty mix of snow and slush gives the Jeep's tires something to grab onto. As long as I take it easy, we should be okay.

After a couple of miles, he takes the lid off of his coffee to get the last drops from the cup and then sighs. "This isn't some kind of spur-of-the-moment plan to kidnap me and hold me for ransom, is it?"

I can hear the humor in his voice, so I give him a fake and highly exaggerated offended look. "Sir, I'll have you know when I kidnap billionaires, I plan that shit."

"Just in case you change your mind, I'm allergic to the adhesive in duct tape."

"I have zip ties in my glove box." I actually do, since my dad thinks everything can be fixed with duct tape,

WD-40, or zip ties. He's not wrong. "Kidnapping you for ransom would be complicated, though. I have nobody to send the ransom demand to. Your assistant's getting married and it would be mean to send it to your mom after she hurt herself on vacation."

"There's all that contact info on the website," he reminds me, and I laugh.

"That's true. I could send them an email through the contact form with my address and cell phone number so they know how to get me the money. I'll just include one of those notices at the bottom telling them the information is confidential and can't be shared."

"That'll work. Nobody *ever* ignores that notice."

I laugh and then take a sip of my coffee. It's cold because I've been clutching the steering wheel instead of drinking it, but at least I still have some. Visibility sucks and it's slow going, so cold caffeine is better than none.

"So where are we going, anyway?" he asks. "Where's home?"

"Charming Lake. It's not much farther."

"You're kidding."

"No really. Maybe five more miles."

"I mean about the whole Charming Lake thing."

"Oh, yeah. It's corny. But in the late 1800s, a rich guy brought his wife up to the White Mountains by train and there was a side trip to the lake. She said it was the most charming spot she'd ever seen, so he bought all the land and named their fancy summer house the Charming Lake House. Then he lost all his money and bits of land got sold off. A small town grew, but everybody still called it Charming Lake."

"That *is* corny."

"Wait until you see our Christmas decorations."

He groans, and I'm not surprised he's rocking that whole Scrooge vibe. The man *is* a billionaire, after all. He probably spends his holiday in his countinghouse with his stacks of gold coins, fuming because his staff has the audacity to want to be with their families.

CHAPTER
Four

Donovan

EVEN WITH THE Jeep's wipers struggling to keep the windshield free of the sleet and freezing rain coming down, it looks like Natalie's driven us to the set of one of those Christmas romance movies my mom and Judy love to watch. They have special coffee mugs and blankets and everything.

They'd certainly love this place. Snow-covered wreaths hanging on every pole. Christmas lights draping from every eave and framing every window. Many of those windows also have electric candles glowing behind the glass, and it wouldn't surprise me at all if the town of Charming Lake piped Christmas carols out through hidden speakers.

"I should warn you there might be a lot of people at the inn when we get there," she says, pulling my attention away from the live-action Christmas card I'm suddenly a part of. "Not regular guests because we're more of a summer town, but the entire family gathers there when something's going on, like preparing for the Christmas parade."

"So that inn is full of your family members right now?" I've watched enough Christmas comedies with my mom to know an entire family gathered under one roof for the holidays will inevitably be a disaster. I'm too tired to be collateral damage in a festive family feud.

"It is. We mostly like each other, though, so it's not as bad as it sounds. Aunt Marilyn can be a little high maintenance, but she's who I was dropping off at the airport."

"Do you live in it full time?" What I really want to know is if she has a husband—despite the lack of a wedding ring—or a boyfriend, but asking might cause her to think I'm interested in her. Which I am, but I don't want *her* to know that.

"Yes, I have a room on the third floor. There are four guest rooms on the second floor and one that's handicap accessible on the first floor. My Nana Jo is staying in that one this weekend."

"Does anybody else live there?"

She laughs, shaking her head. "I'm the youngest of four. After my brother and my sisters moved out, my parents realized they really hate stairs, and they bought a little ranch on the edge of town before I could move out. Last one standing stays."

"Did they ask you first?"

"They didn't have to. I've wanted to run the inn since I was a little girl. I even had my own stool behind the reception desk back when I was too short to see over it."

Interesting. I couldn't wait to get out of the small town where I was born and raised. Of course, I didn't grow up in a charming inn in a charming town on a charming lake. I'm from a mill town with a long-closed mill where there was very little money and not a lot of charm. Most of the residents lived there because they couldn't afford to leave.

"Keep your fingers crossed we make it up the driveway," she says, waving her hands at an enormous Queen Anne house on a hill overlooking the lake. I've spent time in the Hamptons because that's where the summer schmoozing takes place, and this house would almost rival the estate homes there.

I know the Charming Inn probably got its name from being located in the town of Charming Lake, but I have to admit charming's a good word to describe it.

Twinkling white lights are strung along the eaves of the porch that wraps around the front and there's an electric candle glowing in every window, of course. Green garland accented with white lights is looped around the railings of the porch, including the built-in gazebo on the corner, and climbs the supports. A matching wreath graces the door, and the look is welcoming and elegant.

Adding a festive splash of color is a very tall tree in the front yard wrapped in traditional, multicolored Christmas lights.

I don't allow myself to close my eyes or dig my fingernails into the top of the Jeep's door panel as Natalie finesses the vehicle up the untreated drive. I'm not an anxious person by nature, but I'm usually in the backseat of a very large SUV, staring at my phone. Being in the front seat of a small Jeep in a winter storm is hell on the nerves.

When she pulls into a parking spot reserved by a sign proclaiming it's for the employee of the month, I let out the breath I hadn't realized I was holding.

"Employee of the month, huh?"

Natalie laughs. "Yup. For the eighty-third or fourth month in a row."

She hasn't turned off the ignition yet and I don't really care if she does. Now that we're off the roads and safe, I'm in no hurry to go inside. I'd rather sit in the warm Jeep, alone with Natalie.

I don't understand what's happening. Now that we're here, I should call the airport to see if they've found my briefcase. The time between putting the case under the seat and now is the longest I've gone without checking my phone for potential business fires since my first smartphone, and I should be twitching with the need to touch base with my email account. I need to confirm my mom and Judy have returned to the resort safely. I need to regain some semblance of control.

But my muscles have relaxed. I'm calm. And with the twinkling lights reflecting in Natalie's eyes, that drive to work—to push and grind and never let up—seems to have abandoned me for the moment.

Maybe under some other circumstances, I'd be tempted to lean in. To touch her hand and deepen the connection between us. When the time was right, I'd kiss her and free her hair so I could bury my fingers in it.

But the connection's all in my head. The only thing this woman wants from me is one hundred thousand dollars, and I can't let myself forget that.

CHAPTER
Five

Natalie

I CAN TELL from the vehicles in the parking area that most of my family left early, before the storm got bad. But my parents and Nana Jo are still here, as well as my sister Lyla and her two girls. Mel and Elsie are six and four, and once a sleepover at the inn has been promised, not even Mother Nature can retract it.

Usually I go around to the back door, but I have a billionaire with me, so I lead him up the walkway—illuminated by subtle, solar powered lighting—to the front door. Thankfully, it's been freshly salted, probably by my dad, so neither of us fall on our asses. None of us asked Santa for a personal injury lawsuit this year.

"Is everything okay?" Donovan asks, and I realize I'm standing with my hand on the doorknob, looking at him. "You're frowning at me again."

I don't want to confess I was wondering if he'd sue us

if he fell. On the one hand, it's not as if he needs the money. On the other hand, a man doesn't get a billion dollars by leaving money on the table. But he hasn't fallen —I knock on the wooden door to fend off the jinx—so it doesn't matter.

"Sorry. I was thinking about what a skating rink that driveway's going to be in the morning," I lie, and then I push open the door and almost knock the older of my two nieces on her ass.

"Mel! What are you doing?"

"You knocked on the door, so I was going to open it."

"You did knock, which I thought was a little odd since you said you live here," Donovan confirms, and I remember the light rap I'd given the door to ensure our guest didn't fall and bankrupt us.

I don't really have a good reason for knocking I care to share, though, so I lean down to look Mel over. "I didn't bonk you in the head, did I?"

"No bonks." She giggles and then turns her attention to Donovan. "Who died?"

"I..." Donovan stops, clearly confused. "I don't know."

"Nobody died. Funerals are the only time her dad and granddad ever wear a suit like that," I explain. Neither of them actually owns a suit that nice, but I keep that to myself as Elsie runs into the foyer. I give her a quick hug before introducing them to Donovan. "This is Mr. Wilson. And these are my nieces—Mel, who is six, and Elsie is four."

He gives them a dramatic bow that makes them laugh. "It's a pleasure to meet you. I didn't know you could have twins two years apart."

It's not the first time we've heard that joke, but I laugh anyway. "They're both the spitting image of their mother, too. Just be warned, if you mention the strong resemblance in front of my mom, you'll spend your evening looking at every picture she ever took of Lyla when she was their ages. And Mom takes a *lot* of pictures."

"Somebody has to," Mom says as she steps into the foyer, with my dad, grandmother, and sister right behind her. They're probably all curious to hear about the stranger I'd not only let into my Jeep, but brought home with me. "If it had been up to your father, all we'd have to remember your childhoods by would be school pictures and somehow all three of you girls managed to look like you just crawled out of a dumpster after a three-day bender on picture days."

"This is Donovan Wilson, who doesn't need to know *everything* about our lives. He's trying to get to Stowe because his mom was hurt skiing—she's okay—but the weather turned ugly on us. Donovan, my parents—Stella and Randy Byrne—and my sister, Lyla. I don't need to tell you she's Mel and Elsie's mom, of course. And my grandmother, Josephine, who goes by Nana Jo whether she's your nana or not."

"It's nice to meet you all," Donovan says. "I appreciate the hospitality. I left my briefcase on the plane, with my phone and wallet in it, so I was stranded at the airport."

"And now you're stranded in Charming Lake," Mom says. "There are worse places to be."

"You put your wallet in your briefcase?" Dad asks, and then he grunts when Mom elbows him in the side.

"I won't do it again," Donovan says easily. "Luckily, Natalie rescued me."

"Natalie loves to bring home strays, and this is much better than the time she brought home the stray raccoon." Donovan gives me a questioning look, and I roll my eyes. My parents have worked Robby the Raccoon into a surprising number of conversations over the years, and I'm tired of hearing about him. "You two must be hungry. Everybody's going in the TV room to watch Christmas movies while wrapping gifts for the Santa Fund kids, but you go sit in the dining room and I'll bring you plates."

I notice Donovan doesn't seem to have a problem with being bossed around by my mother. I doubt being told what to do is a big part of his personality, but if he went straight from a business meeting to a plane, he probably hasn't had a decent meal in a while.

It's hard to say if he's going to have a decent meal now or not. It depends on who made it, since we're mediocre cooks at best. My mom's friend freelance cooks for us if we have guests who request meals, but there's a reason we're an inn and not a bed-and-breakfast. Nobody's handing out stars for cold cereal and over-toasted bagels.

I guess it's Donovan's lucky day because not only did he get rescued by a woman who owns a four-wheel-drive and an inn, but Mom carries two plates of Nana Jo's lasagna into the dining room. Of all the Byrne women, she's the best in the kitchen, but it's a low bar.

"Thank you," Donovan says when she sets a plate in front of him. "I was going to ask to borrow your phone to let my mother know I'm off the roads for the night, but this smells amazing."

I slide my phone toward him. "You can send her a text if you want. It's a pretty formal dining room, but no guests means no rules."

"Thank you, but I'll just wait and call her. Once a text exchange with my mom is started, it's hard to get out of. Same with a phone call, actually."

"Oh!" Mom was almost out of the dining room, but now she turns back. "You don't have your phone."

"It's in my briefcase with my wallet," Donovan reminds her, his fork in midair because he was about to take his first bite of lasagna.

"I have that prepaid cell phone Marilyn bought to harass…" My mom hesitates, leaving a few awkward seconds of silence before she rallies. "The one she bought before she lost her husband. I just charged it, too, because I was thinking about giving it to somebody who might need it. Let me get it from the kitchen."

As soon as Mom leaves the room, Donovan turns to me with a small crease between his eyebrows I think might be permanent. He really needs to relax more. "Are there going to be text messages in that phone that could get me in trouble?"

"No. When the police chief knocked on her door, my aunt locked herself in the bathroom and deleted all the texts. She thought that would make them disappear from the other woman's phone, too." I sigh, shaking my head. "She got a stern talking to, and she was extra embarrassed because she dumped the police chief to hook up with my uncle back in the day, so there's some history and an unusually high number of parking tickets between those two. But she stopped contacting the other woman. The phone is safe."

He looks like he has more questions, but Mom returns and holds a small black device out to him. In her other hand is the charging cord and a prepaid card for the phone. When he takes it and flips it open—because of course it's a flip-phone—I brace myself for his reaction. The man undoubtedly owns the fanciest, most up-to-date tech on the market, and this phone is *not* that. It doesn't even have a screen with a keyboard, and composing a single text message will probably take him at least fifteen minutes.

It's probably a good thing it flips closed into a compact size because if he insults it and hurts my mother's feelings, I'm going to shove that phone up his—

"Thank you," he says. "I really appreciate this. I know you have the landline here, but it's hard for me, feeling disconnected. Especially from my mom."

Oh. So he isn't a *total* jerk.

"I put a sticky note with the phone number on the back of this card," Mom says, handing him the accessories. "And my number and Natalie's number are on there, too."

"This means a lot to me," he says, and my mom beams. "Really. Thank you."

Then she leaves us alone to eat, and neither of us talk. I hadn't realized how hungry I was until Mom set the plate in front of me. I'm also distracted by the noises coming from Donovan's end of the table. They're somewhere between a humming sound and a moan, and I know they're showing his appreciation for Nana Jo's lasagna. If I close my eyes, though, it's way too easy to imagine him making those same sounds in my bed.

As soon as I swallow the last bite of my lasagna, I stand and gather my dirty dishes. "I'll be right back. And do not even think about clearing your own place. It might kill my mother."

"I'm not a guest. I mean, not a *paying* guest," he says. "Yet."

"It doesn't matter. Guests, paying or otherwise, do *not* help."

I walk out before he can argue with me. I couldn't care less if he clears his plate or not, but I need a few minutes away from him—away from the noises he made and the way I can't stop myself from looking at him. It's just my luck that Mom hasn't joined the rest of the family in the TV room, so once she realizes Donovan isn't behind me, she snaps my butt with the end of the dish towel.

"He sure is a handsome one," she says.

"Yup." There's no way I'm telling her he's also rich. She might lock him in a closet and refuse to let him leave until he's put a ring on my finger. "He was really worried about his mom, but thankfully he was able to talk to her and find out it's just a sprained ankle before I had to tell him we weren't going to make it there."

"You can tell a lot about a man by how he cares for his mother."

Donovan *definitely* cares for his mother. The man is willing to pay me a hundred thousand dollars to drive him to Vermont in a blizzard because she hurt herself skiing, not that I'll share that detail with my mom. Sure, he seems like a nice guy now that he knows his mother isn't fighting for her life in some rural hospital, but there's still a chance he'll forget about the deal he'd made with me two seconds after the town disappears from his rearview mirror. Until I have that money in my hand, I'm not getting anybody's hopes up.

"It's a magical time," Mom continues, giving me a side-eye that makes me nervous. "Maybe a Christmas miracle brought him for you."

"Super flattered you think it'll take a Christmas miracle to find me a husband. And also, no." Absolutely not. Sure, just looking at him makes my heart race and certain parts of my body ache to be touched, but he's a billionaire.

Maybe that should go in the plus column, rather than the minus, but it's not so much about the money. It's about the lifestyle that goes with the money. Donovan's undoubtedly a workaholic. His mother even teased him about never putting down his phone. It would be business first, and maybe there's a few spare moments for a personal life, or maybe there isn't. Travel. Fancy dinners. Entitled, manipulative people.

I'm a small-town girl, and my heart belongs to my family and my Charming Lake community. It doesn't matter if Santa himself put Donovan in my path and had his elves abscond with his briefcase—a man like that's not for me.

CHAPTER
Six

Donovan

OF COURSE I tell Natalie to precede me up the stairs. Ladies first and all that, plus she knows where we're going. It makes sense.

What doesn't make sense is my inability to take my eyes off her ass as she climbs the steps. I'm usually a lot better at controlling my libido—at shoving down desire for a woman who'll be a complicated distraction.

I prefer short, uncomplicated flings that don't distract me from my businesses. And the women I get involved with want exactly the same thing from me. Maybe some nice dinners. Plus-ones at an event or two. A few orgasms. No expectations.

Natalie has expectations. She expects a big payout for a little kindness, which is something I can't allow myself to forget.

"This is you," she says when we reach the last door on the left.

I'm not sure what I was expecting—a lot of florals and ruffles, maybe—but the room is simple and elegant in neutral cream colors with sage and blue accents. The furniture, including a wardrobe and small writing desk, is done in the Shaker style, and I can practically feel myself relaxing.

Until Natalie brushes my arm on her way to the other side of the room.

I'm alone with her again, and I know I should be listening as she points out the features and quirks of the room I'll be spending the night in, but it's hard to concentrate on the remote control and thermostat.

"The underwear is new, though. Don't worry."

"Excuse me?" I clearly missed something. "What about underwear?"

"The packages aren't even open." I'm about to ask her *what package* because I have no idea why we're talking about underwear, but she points to a basket I hadn't noticed on the floor, next to the wardrobe.

It appears to be folded clothing, and on top of the pile sits two packages—one of what appears to be men's white briefs and the other white crew socks.

"The underwear isn't used is what I'm saying," Natalie continues. "That would be weird."

Or *more* weird, at least. "Do you keep a variety of socks and underwear on hand for your guests?"

She laughs. "No. They're my dad's Christmas gift from my mother. To make a long story short, in 2016, Dad bought Mom an iron and a car vacuum for Christmas and since then, she's refused to give him anything but socks and underwear for Christmas."

I nod because I've never even had a wife and I know he asked for that. "I don't want to take his Christmas presents, though. Such as they are."

"Mom buys during sales and stuff, and she has a stockpile. Even without these, I think Dad will find underwear under the tree for at least eight more years." She shrugs. "And the clothes…those are not new. Mom says you're roughly the same size as my sister's ex. Lyla put a bunch of boxes in the attic, including some of his stuff, so Mom found you a few things. A little dusty, maybe, but it was clean when it went up there."

"I appreciate it."

"I know it's probably not what you're used to," she says, looking around as if trying to see the room through my eyes. Then she snorts. "Not *probably.* It's *definitely* not what you're used to, but after the day you've had, I think you'll sleep well."

Or I might lie awake thinking about her all night. "The room is perfect. And without you, I'd probably be trying to sleep sitting up straight in an airport chair, so I really do appreciate everything you're doing."

"If you need anything, just call me. You can also text, of course, if it's not urgent and you have a lot more patience with cycling through number keys than I do."

We both laugh, and then she lingers, as if she has something else to say. Or maybe as though she's waiting for me to say something. But what can I say? I certainly can't tell her I'd like for her to hang out longer so I can get to know her better—a *lot* better.

"Goodnight, Donovan," she says, and then she's gone before I can say anything at all.

It's probably for the best.

The adrenaline that's kept me going all day—from

getting the news Mom was hurt through the rush to get on a flight, losing my phone and wallet, and the drive through the storm—is seeping out of me and all I want to do is stretch out on the bed and close my eyes.

But first I need to call Mom from the cell phone Stella lent to me. I'd text her, but I've had a long day and cycling through numbers trying to find letters isn't in my current skill set.

Once I've explained where I am, and why, I can hear the relief in her voice.

"I'm so glad you're off the roads, honey. They're bad, I hear, and getting worse by the minute. The resort is totally booked, too. You were going to have to sleep on the sofa in our suite."

"Not exactly ideal," I admit.

"Especially during our anniversary trip," Mom adds, and she doesn't sound as if she's one hundred percent teasing. "This works out perfectly because you can relax for the weekend and we'll have our driver stop by and pick you up on our way to the airport."

It takes a few seconds for her words to sink in, and then I don't know what to say. They're going to stop and get me on their way through? They were checking out and flying back on *Sunday*. It's Thursday. Natalie's planning to drive me the rest of the way tomorrow, when the storm's over, and I don't know how she's going to feel about fronting me a room for two extra nights.

But there's no room at the resort, and I absolutely don't want to crash Mom and Judy's anniversary trip.

Once I'm off the phone, I rummage through the basket of borrowed clothes. They're definitely not fashion choices I would make for myself, but they're clean and I'm surprised to see they *will* probably fit me. There's a pair of sweatpants, so I strip out of my suit and take a long, hot shower.

I don't remember my head hitting the pillow, but the next thing I know, sunlight is streaming into the room and I'm wide awake. I also feel surprisingly refreshed, probably a combination of yesterday's rollercoaster and an excellent mattress.

I'm more of a black boxer brief guy, but I open the package of white briefs and pull a pair of jeans and a blue flannel shirt out of the basket. My shoes definitely don't vibe with the flannel, so I pull on the socks and figure I'll worry about footwear later. Right now, finding coffee is a lot higher on my priority list.

I step into the hall and turn toward the stairs, only to stop short with a strangled sound of surprise stuck in my throat. Not a scream, of course. More like a grunt.

There are two little girls standing side-by-side at the end of the hall, and it's only after every image of twins from that horror movie that scared the shit out of me when I was a kid goes through my head that I place them as Natalie's nieces.

Mel and Elsie, though I can't remember which is which with my heart still hammering and my mouth dry. I may be the baddest guy in any boardroom, but a *very* enthusiastic fear of ghosts took hold of me at a young age, and I've never shaken it. I've got nerves of steel until somebody breaks out a Ouija board and then there's a whooshing sound and a me-shaped hole in the wall.

"Good morning," I say, pretty proud of how steady my voice is.

"Nana Jo says breakfast is ready," the taller of the two girls says.

Mel, I think. My brain's starting to recover from the

adrenaline spike. "Thank you. I was just on my way down."

Just then, Natalie appears at the top of the stairs, slightly flushed and breathless, and my mind goes blank again.

"Girls," she hisses. "You know better."

Elsie puts her hands on her hips. "Nana Jo said to tell mister…that man, that breakfast is ready."

"Nana Jo is not the boss here. I am, and you both know you're not allowed to be up here alone when there's a guest. And Mister *that man* is a guest." I clear my throat and her cheeks turn a darker shade of pink. "Also, his name is Mr. Wilson."

"Donovan is fine, unless there's a hard rule against it."

"There is. And since you're up, you should come eat," Natalie says as the girls push past her and run down the stairs. "No running!"

"They're cute kids," I say once they're gone—though I can hear their footsteps on the wood floor downstairs and they're definitely still running. I have no intention of telling her they just terrified me.

"Being cute is why they get away with so much." She waits as I pull the door to my room closed and walk toward her. "I should warn you, though, that there are several reasons why the sign says *inn* and not *bed-and-breakfast*, but the most important one is that we try to avoid offering food to guests as much as possible."

I'm surprised she's admitting that out loud. "Food service can definitely play hell on the profit margins."

"What? Oh…no. We're not great at that cooking thing."

"The lasagna last night was good." Granted, I'd been starving and I've admittedly had better, but it wasn't bad.

She shrugs. "We each have one dish we can make passably well."

"Really? What's yours?"

"I make a mean microwave pizza."

I laugh as she turns toward the stairs, but then she stops and looks back at me. Her gaze is intense, and for a second I think she might say something…intimate. Something like asking me how I slept and then telling me she couldn't sleep at all because she was thinking about sneaking to my room and…

Then the corners of her mouth tilt up. "Nice outfit."

"I got it from *your* family, so technically you picked it out."

"Yeah, my sister divorced him, so…" She chuckles. "Might have been that shirt."

CHAPTER
Seven

Natalie

LEADING Donovan into the dining room to find my mom dishing scrambled eggs onto everybody's plate is a huge relief. Scrambled eggs are pretty hard to screw up, even for us, so Donovan's going two-for-two on edible meals.

"Good morning," everybody says at once.

"Good morning," Donovan replies, sitting in the empty chair I wave him toward.

The coffee carafe on his end of the table gets his immediate attention, so thankfully he's not looking when Nana Jo slides into the chair I was about to sit in. I'm confused because I always sit there, until she not-so-subtly jerks her head toward the empty chair next to Donovan.

Oh, hell. Either the matchmaking bug is contagious or my mother and grandmother have put their heads together and are deliberately scheming to get me close to Donovan. I'm not sure which option is worse.

I glare at Nana Jo, shaking my head. She ignores me, smiling at our guest instead of moving. "How did you sleep last night, Donovan?"

He pauses, coffee cup halfway to his mouth. "I had one of the best night's sleep I've had in a long time. I was very comfortable, thank you."

"That's what we like to hear," my dad says from the head of the table. "Not that I'm surprised. Our Natalie always exceeds our expectations."

And my dad's in on it, too. Naturally, Donovan looks over at me, which keeps me from rolling my eyes, but my family's ridiculous. They don't even know our guest is totally loaded. They just see an attractive man in a nice suit and they're ready to offer me up like I'm a complimentary gift.

They should rethink that strategy because if I run off with a billionaire, my parents either have to take the day-to-day running of the inn back on, or leave Lyla to run it. I love my sister—and my nieces—but they're a little chaotic for the hospitality business.

Thankfully, there's a lot on the family to-do list for the day, so there's more eating than talking. I notice Donovan doesn't seem to mind the over-done bacon and under-done English muffins served with the scrambled eggs, but he definitely likes the coffee. He's on his third cup—with no cream or sugar, which makes me shudder—when my father pushes back from the table.

"Guess I should start the storm clean-up," he says. "It's going to take me a while."

His exit starts a chain reaction of family members having something pressing they have to do. To be fair, the day before the town Christmas fair is *always* hectic, but the fact they've left me alone in the dining room with Donovan doesn't escape me.

"Should I put another pot on?" I ask when I see him pouring the last coffee from both carafes into his cup.

"Not yet," he says, picking up the cup. "I think I'm still under-caffeinated from yesterday. And I'm not a big breakfast eater, but I go through more coffee than I should."

"There's a Keurig in the kitchen. You're welcome to use it." I stand, preparing to clear the table since that job's obviously been left to me. I'm surprised when Donovan stands and picks up his plate. "You can leave that. Just drink your coffee and I'll take care of this."

"I can help." I'm about to remind him he's a guest when he shakes his head. "Customer's always right, you know."

I snort. "I think that's for *paying* customers."

He just laughs and starts gathering dirty dishes. It takes several trips, and on the last trip to the kitchen, he brings his coffee cup, which is still half full. "So, I have a little problem."

I straighten from the dishwasher rack I'm loading, arching an eyebrow at him. "Thread count not to your satisfaction?"

"The sheets are fine. Better than fine, actually. It's a comfortable bed, and I didn't want to get out of it this morning."

"Okay, so what's the problem? Do you need a doctor?" I lower my voice and lean close. "Is it a rash?"

"I do *not* have a rash," he says, and then he must realize he said it loudly because he looks around to see if anybody was nearby. "My mother and her wife are in Stowe celebrating their wedding anniversary and there are no available rooms. All she could come up with was the sofa in the living room of their suite."

"That's no fun for them."

He snorts. "Not exactly a good time for me, either. But my mom suggested that I just stay here and relax, and they'll swing by and pick me up on their way to the airport on Sunday."

I've worked in hospitality for too long to let the smile slip, but Sunday? It's Friday. That's a lot of time to be around this man. When I can forget that he lives some high-powered billionaire life somewhere and probably does nothing but bark orders at people around the clock, he's irresistible.

"Is that a problem?" he asks, probably because I've been silently thinking about how much I want to run my fingers through that hair. And of course my imagination didn't stop there, so I don't know how long the awkward silence has stretched on. "I can figure something out if it's not okay."

I'm not sure what kind of options a man with no car, no wallet and no phone thinks he's going to do in a small town in the middle of nowhere with the roads still a mess. His mom could help him, though. She could make arrangements with her own credit cards from Stowe, including sending a car service to pick him up. Hell, she could send a car to take him back to the airport or to drive him back to New York.

But she's celebrating her anniversary, so he probably doesn't want to take up her time. And even though I know it's a bad idea because I'm not great at resisting temptation, I want him to stay.

"Of course it's okay," I say, and he visibly relaxes. "On one condition."

His slow smile suggests his mind has gone to a place I wouldn't mind exploring. *You can stay, but only if you stay in my bed.* Or maybe *you can stay, but only if you're naked.*

As if I'd have the nerve to say either of those things, even though I'd like to.

"What's the condition?" he prompts.

"You can't hide in your room. This is the weekend Charming Lake celebrates Christmas, and you have to embrace it."

I'm not sure why it matters to me. It's certainly best for my imagination and my neglected sex drive if he stays in his room for the duration. My attraction to the uptight guy in the expensive suit has nothing on how much I want this version of him—relaxed in denim and flannel, with that flare of heat in his eyes every time he looks at me.

"With you as my Charming Lake holiday guide?" he asks, and I see too late how I've cornered myself.

"Of course." I don't see any way to say no.

I can't look away as his lips curve into a smile that makes me feel like prey he's toying with—but in a good way. "Spending the weekend with you? I can embrace that."

CHAPTER *Eight*

Donovan

I DON'T KNOW why I'm torturing myself. Assuming I can find better footwear, there's no reason I can't wander around Charming Lake alone. There's no good reason to spend the weekend in close proximity to Natalie.

Close enough to smell her hair. To feel the warmth radiating from her. Itching to touch her. Listening to her laugh and the warmth in her voice. Watching her mouth and wondering what kissing her would feel like.

Okay, I do know why I'm torturing myself. Bad idea or not, I can't stop myself from wanting her. And judging by the way she keeps looking at me, her eyes sweeping up and down my body and her bottom lip caught between her teeth, she's not against the idea, either.

Having a fling with the person I'm dependent on for literally everything right now would be a bad idea. But, like many bad ideas, it would really feel good while it lasted.

I'm about to take a step or two closer to her—to test her reaction—when her grandmother walks into the kitchen.

"Natalie, did your dad—" She stops, blinking at him. "Oh. I didn't expect to find you in here."

"I insisted," I say, just so there's no confusion. "Since the inn is closed for Christmas, I'm not technically a guest. I'm more like a..."

I stop talking because I can't think of a word to fill in that blank.

"Like a *guest*?" Jo supplies, and then she laughs. "I know what you mean."

"Did my dad what?" Natalie asks.

"Oh, did he tell you the plow went by a few minutes ago?"

"He didn't. I heard it, though. Thanks."

Nana Jo turns her attention back to me. "What do you do for work, Donovan?"

I glance at Natalie, and she gives an almost imperceptible shake of her head. I'm not sure if she's trying to tell me she hasn't told my family who I am, or if she doesn't want them to know.

"I'm in real estate," I say, and it's not actually a lie.

"Interesting," she says. "I like to go to open houses because I'm nosy and sometimes they have cookies. Do you put cookies out?"

I try to imagine an open house with pastries for an eight or nine figure piece of commercial property and smile. "I don't, but that's an excellent idea that I'll share with my team. Every business deal should involve cookies."

Nana Jo gives me a big smile before disappearing again, and Natalie goes back to loading the dishwasher.

I'm not sure what the significance is of the plow going by. Obviously it means the roads are reasonably passable, but maybe Natalie's grandmother had been hinting that they could get rid of the stranger she'd brought home.

"That was nice of you," Natalie says. "Not laughing at her, I mean."

Ouch. "Just because I have a lot of money doesn't mean I'm a horrible person, you know."

The sound she makes is straight skepticism, but I can't really blame her. Most of the people with that much money make the news or social media for not great reasons. And there are very few people I'm involved in business with that I'd want around my family.

Rather than try to convince her I'm a decent guy with a knack for making money, I take over the job of scraping the plates so she can put them in the dishwasher. We work in silence for a few minutes, and it feels good. If somebody looked through the window, we'd look like a regular couple just cleaning the kitchen together, and I'm taken aback by how badly I wish that was true.

"I'm shocked you know how to do that," she says as she takes the last plate from me.

That hurts, which surprises me. I usually don't care what anybody except my mom, Judy, and my closest advisors think of me. But it bothers me that Natalie thinks I'm incapable of doing basic household chores. "I can do a lot of things that would surprise you."

"Your mom said you don't even drive yourself. Last night, I was waiting for you to ask if we provide a valet to squeeze just the right amount of toothpaste onto your toothbrush for you." She laughs when I give her a sideways look.

"I used to love driving," I say, not sure why I feel compelled to share that. "I gave it up a long time ago because it was a waste of time."

"If you loved doing it, it wasn't a waste of your time."

"I was fighting Manhattan traffic, trying to get back into the city for a meeting with an investor and I was frustrated because I could be using that time to prepare for the meeting I had after that one. I started thinking about how much time I spent driving that could be spent working in the backseat and decided a driver made more sense from a business standpoint."

"There's more to life than business," she says, and my body tenses in response.

"No," I say immediately, a reflexive rejection of that idea.

She gives me a disappointed look that I feel to my core. "Yes."

With anybody else, I'd probably freeze them with a look and move on, but I can't do it. "My companies employ hundreds of people. There are investors. A lot of people depend on me giving them one hundred percent. I take that responsibility very seriously and I can't fail."

She tilts her head, and I can see that she's not going to let it go. "How much of your money is generational wealth?"

"None. I earned every dollar."

"Okay, so you must be pretty smart." Somehow it doesn't sound like she's trying to flatter me. "I bet you've hired a lot of really smart people to help you, right?"

"The best."

"So I think you can probably take a weekend for yourself without all of those companies crumbling." She grins. "Plus, you don't have any choice because you put your phone and wallet in your briefcase and then lost the briefcase. And now you're stuck with me, so you may as well let yourself enjoy it."

I don't tell her that's exactly what I want to do—I *want* to let myself enjoy being stuck with her—but I can't lose sight of why she's doing this. One hundred thousand dollars.

She's right. I *am* smart. I have self-discipline and willpower. And my brain is in charge, not my dick. I'll be keeping that in my borrowed denim pants.

CHAPTER
Nine

Natalie

"YOU SAID your dish is microwave pizza."

"I lied." I slap Donovan's hand when he reaches for the pie plate. He's already had a slice of the apple pie. He cut it himself and to say it was a generous serving would be an understatement. "I'm pretty good at baking, which is different from cooking. The kids can use my burgers as hockey pucks, but pies and breads, I can do. Cookies are iffy."

I've spent most of the morning in the kitchen, baking and preparing food. Donovan disappeared for a little while to call his mom and check in with the airport on the status of his lost briefcase. And then he got roped into helping Mel and Elsie build an absolutely disastrous gingerbread house so Lyla could help Mom with decorations for the inn's parade float.

But when he snuck into the kitchen for another cup of coffee, he sat on a stool at the island to watch me cutting a pie and he hasn't left yet. Donovan watching makes me a little self-conscious, but I do like his company.

"What's in those dishes?" he asks, pointing at four small, covered casserole dishes on the counter.

"Lasagna, and it's not for you."

"Your family really likes lasagna."

"Nana Jo enjoys making it. There's a bit of a difference. And it travels well."

That gets his attention. "Where's it going?"

"To a few neighbors who don't have family in town, but don't get around well in this weather. You'll get to see Charming Lake in the daylight." He's frowning, and I give him a look. "You said you'd embrace the holiday spirit, remember?"

"I didn't exactly pack for holiday spirit of the outdoor variety."

"You would have left it on the plane, anyway," I tease, and then I realize what he's saying. "We can find you some boots."

His face scrunches up and it's adorable. "Great."

"You're already wearing borrowed clothes and my dad's underwear," I remind him. "Boots are nothing."

He holds up a finger. "Just to clarify, the package of underwear was unopened, and it was a Christmas gift that hadn't yet been gifted. So technically, I'm not wearing *your father's* underwear."

I laugh at him while pulling a collapsible tote out of the pantry. Once I've carefully loaded it with the casserole dishes, I add four individually packaged slices of the pie in containers with the inn's name written on them. Leftover containers being cycled back to their original owners is something of a sport in Charming Lake.

"Let's find you some boots," I say, and he groans as he pushes off the stool. I'm not sure if it's a reluctance to go or the amount of pie he ate.

My dad's backup boots are slightly loose on him, but it's better than being too tight. Once I've snagged him a coat and gloves, he's out of excuses. He waits patiently, holding the casseroles, while I put on my coat and boots.

I should probably take the tote because I have more experience walking outside in the snow than he does, but I already know he'll be stubborn about it. Chivalry and all that. I lead the way to the Jeep, thankful my dad was diligent about clearing and salting the walkways. We didn't need our guest breaking his butt, and we *definitely* don't want him to break the casserole dishes.

"This tote smells delicious," he says.

"You just ate a third of a pie."

"I had *one* slice."

"A slice that barely fit on the plate."

"It was a small plate."

He clearly isn't going to admit he put away an almost indecent amount of my apple pie, so I open the back door of the Jeep so he can set the tote on the backseat.

"You should drive," I say, surprising us both. I hadn't planned it that way, but it felt right in the moment.

He frowns, obviously confused. "You mean right now?"

"We could stand out here until frostbite sets in, but now would probably be better."

"But why?"

"Because you used to enjoy driving and it'll be fun."

He doesn't look convinced. "I called Bob earlier and the roads will be fine for the Jeep."

"Who's Bob?"

"The plow guy."

"I don't have my license on me."

"We're not leaving town, and even if Jace pulled us over—which he won't because he knows my Jeep—he won't give you a ticket."

"Who is Jace, and why won't he pull you over?"

"He's the police officer on duty and he won't pull me over because he's my sister's ex-boyfriend. Also, because I don't give him a reason to."

"A rule follower, huh?"

There's no sneer to his tone, but his words still sound like a challenge. And I can see that he wants to drive—it's written all over his face. "Seems to me you're the one hung up on the rules right now. And before you try to use the weather as an excuse, it's a beautiful day. And everybody will be going extra slow because of the roads, so we'll be perfectly safe in the Jeep."

"I get to choose the radio station," he says, catching the keys I toss to him.

I laugh at him while sliding into the passenger seat. "Nope. It's Christmas music or silence."

"The driver picks the music. Everybody knows that."

I wait until he's *very* slowly and cautiously guiding the Jeep down the driveway, both hands clutching the steering wheel, and then switch the media input to my phone so an upbeat Christmas dance tune plays through the speakers.

I watch him glance at the control screen, but he's too busy trying to drive to figure out how to turn it back to the radio.

"You win." He stops at the bottom of the driveway,

turning his blinker on when I point to the right. But before he pulls out, he gives me a look that promises he's going to get back at me for winning the music fight. "For now."

I'm not sure what punishment he has in mind, but I'm definitely going to enjoy imagining the possibilities.

CHAPTER *Ten*

Donovan

I DON'T KNOW what to make of Natalie Byrne. She's a woman who saw a stranger in distress a week before Christmas and demanded one hundred thousand dollars to help—for a two and a half hour drive.

She's also a woman whose family is incredibly generous with their hospitality. She's smart and funny and warm, and she delivers meals to people who can't get around in bad weather. Sure, I told her I have a lot of money. But nothing about her says she'll take advantage of a person just because she can.

"Pull in here." I do as I'm told, parking in front of a quaint and festively decked out general store. "I'll be right back."

I hum along to a Christmas song the world seems to play every fifteen minutes from early November through

December every year. And while I wait, I think about what I'd usually be doing in a vehicle.

I'd be sitting in the backseat, reading email or reports. Perhaps I'd schedule a call so it wouldn't take up my time in the office. There would be no stops—my drivers arrive with full gas tanks and don't deviate from the most efficient way to reach my destination.

I wouldn't be humming a holiday pop song, that's for sure. Or tapping out the drumbeat on the steering wheel, not feeling any sense of urgency or impatience. It would be easy to say it's because I've been forcibly disconnected from my business, but I don't think that's true. I think it's Natalie.

I could be sitting in front of the television, watching a financial news channel. I know the inn has at least one laptop, since I saw it on an antique table I think serves as their reception desk.

I could have asked for internet access and found a way to get through to my team. Hell, my mom has a black card. The storm was over when I got out of bed and there's no reason I'm not already on my way back to the city.

No reason except the woman walking out of the Charming Lake General Store with a cardboard coffee cup in each hand. Some part of my brain has given me permission to pretend I'm truly stranded in this town with Natalie, and I'm good with that.

I reach across the Jeep and pull the door handle, giving it a shove so she can catch the door with her knee. She hands one cup to me and slides into her seat. Then she closes her door against the cold and the rich aroma of coffee fills the Jeep.

"I know it's been at least two whole hours since you've

had caffeine," she says in a teasing voice. "It's just plain coffee, but it's the best coffee in town."

"Thank you." I risk burning my mouth to take a sip and she's right. It's damn good coffee.

As we drive back to the inn, Natalie points out exceptionally merry decorations and tells me about the time the town tried to ban inflatables on the basis they're too tacky for an elegant, historic town.

"They failed the first time, and they announced they were putting it back on the agenda. Inflatables went up everywhere. I don't even know how much people spent on them, but all you could see from the town hall windows were inflatables. And there was an anonymous note letting them know that every time they tried to vote on it, ten percent more inflatables would be added."

"I noticed Charming Lake seems to love blow-up decorations."

"There were three in the entire town when the debate began."

She shares more stories about the town, and I'm laughing when I pull into her parking spot at the inn. I think I've laughed more since meeting Natalie than I have in months, and my stomach muscles actually ache a little.

The rest of the day passes quickly as I help whoever needs help with their Christmas fair prep. I help Randy string the fishing line across the framework they'd built on the float for the inn. There will be paper snowflakes hanging from it, and I make a couple of those before we all have to admit I'm terrible at making paper snowflakes.

I play a board game with the girls while Lyla goes to help their other sister, Erin, put some finishing touches on the library float. Their brother, Rob, is too busy at the fire station to help, and I hear a lot of complaining about that from Stella.

I don't mind any of it. Not only do I get to see enough of Natalie to make it worthwhile, but I enjoy the family dynamic. Christmas for me means a nice dinner at Mom and Judy's home. They do Christmas Eve with Judy's kids and grandkids and then have a quiet Christmas morning alone. When I show up, we exchange gifts and then have a meal they insist on making themselves.

The noisy chaos of the Byrne family should be overwhelming, but I enjoy being a part of it. Not as much when I choke down overcooked steak with a side of undercooked potatoes, but it's a small price to pay for the apple crisp Natalie brings out for dessert.

After dinner, they gather in the sitting room to decorate the Christmas tree as a family. I try to excuse myself, thinking I'll find a book somewhere and go read in my room, but Mel and Elsie are so disappointed I won't get to see every ornament, I give in.

It's not until Randy's put the star on top and they've taken a million pictures that I get a chance to be alone with Natalie again. The others have all gone back to the event barn to finish the floats, and she volunteered us to clean the kitchen.

I like cleaning the kitchen with Natalie.

We talk mostly about the girls and the floats while we work, but when we're finished, she leans against the island and crosses her arms. "Tell me something."

"Anything." She chuckles, and I give her a look. "Almost anything."

"Why are you single?" She blinks and then holds up a hand. "Wait. You *are* single, right? I mean, you haven't mentioned calling a girlfriend or wife, so I just assumed. Maybe I shouldn't have."

"I'm single. I've had a few girlfriends, but never a wife."

"But *why?*"

I laugh, not sure what she's trying to find out. "I don't know. I'm a busy man."

"There must be packs of women who want to be Mrs. Donovan Wilson."

There are packs of women who want access to my money, but I'm not sure any of them care about *me,* and I'm not willing to settle just to have a beautiful woman gracing my home. And since Natalie's charging me six figures for this adventure—not counting any additional charges I've accrued since arriving at the inn—she should know about that.

I don't like being reminded of our agreement, though, and I want to leave the topic behind.

"I came close once," I tell her. "I was planning to propose to my girlfriend at Christmas. She was fierce when it came to business. We had the same goals in life and together, we were going to be unstoppable. Then she went back to her small hometown to help her grandmother save her house from foreclosure, and she fell in love with some guy who runs his family's Christmas tree farm. Now they live in the house with her grandmother, and she opened a cupcake shop."

It isn't easy to keep a straight face when her eyes widen and her mouth falls open. "Are you serious? That's awful!"

"Very awful," I say in a solemn voice.

Then her eyes narrow. "Wait. I think I saw that movie. You're lying, aren't you?"

"Yes, I'm lying."

She laughs and reaches out to give my shoulder a playful push. I catch her wrist and tug. She's off balance and stumbles, and when I wrap my arm around her to steady her, her body ends up pressed against mine.

Her head tilts back, so she's looking up at me. And she makes no effort to pull back. "I almost believed you."

"My mom and her wife love those Christmas romance movies. I've sat through enough of them to be convincing."

When her hand slides from my upper arm around to the back of my shoulder, I can't resist anymore.

Natalie's mouth is soft and her lips part under mine. *Finally*, I think, because it feels as if I've been waiting to kiss this woman almost from the moment we met. I cup the back of her neck with one hand, while the other presses against her lower back, and deepen the kiss.

"Aunt Natalie!"

I hear the little girl's voice, followed by the thumping of running footsteps, and break off the kiss. Natalie takes a step away, and I move to the back of the island in case the result of getting my hands on Natalie is visible in these jeans.

Mel bursts into the kitchen and I wonder if these girls ever walk, or if they only have the one speed. I don't have a lot of experience being around kids, but if these two are typical, it explains why the parents I know always look exhausted.

"Isn't it past your bedtime?" Natalie asks, and I can hear the frustration in her voice, though Mel doesn't seem to notice.

"Mommy said we can stay up late to help because she's too tired to put us to bed. And Nana Jo says you have to help us with the snowflakes for the float or we'll never get it done."

Natalie sighs. "This would be a lot easier if we didn't pick a new theme every year."

"But it would be boring. Nobody would look at the float if they saw it last year."

"She has a point," I say, earning a stern look from Natalie.

"The point is that I get to stay up late helping make snowflakes." She blows out a breath and then looks at her niece, who looks anxious now. Maybe because her aunt doesn't seem as excited about the prospect as she is. "Okay, let's make snowflakes. Donovan, do you need anything before I go?"

Our eyes meet and she must read my mind because her cheeks get pink. But I'm not going to tease her in front of a kid. "I think I'll go to my room and take a cold shower. Maybe watch some TV."

Mel had started tugging on Natalie's hand, but she stops to frown at me. "Why don't you use hot water?"

"Okay, let's go," Natalie says, heading toward the door. "See you bright and early in the morning, Donovan."

I'm disappointed it doesn't sound as if she's going to sneak into my room when her snowflake duties are over, so it takes a few seconds for her words to sink in. "Wait. Bright and early?"

"Tomorrow's Christmas fair day, and the girls wake up early and very excited about it."

Something to look forward to after a long, restless night imagining all the ways that kiss could have ended if we'd been alone.

CHAPTER
Eleven

Natalie

THE MORNING of the Christmas fair is always chaotic, and it seems worse this year. Maybe it's because I stayed awake too long thinking about that kiss in the kitchen. Then I spent some time working up the nerve to go creeping through the house, only to find there was no light shining under his door.

I didn't want to wake him, so I went back to bed and laid awake some more.

Because it's going to be a long day and there will be a lot of junk food later, my dad makes pancakes. They're *very* dense and filling, so it will be a while before any of us are hungry again.

When it's time to go, I find Donovan in the sitting room, standing with his hands in his pockets. He's looking at the tree and the twinkling lights are reflected in his eyes.

"Do you have one of those magazine trees?" I ask, and

he startles slightly. He'd obviously been deep in thought. "You know, the ones that are twelve feet tall and perfectly symmetrical, with tasteful white glass balls?"

"I haven't had a tree in years." He smiles. "But if I did, I'd want it to be like this one."

"A hot mess of mismatched ornaments, some of which are more glue than glass?"

"The story of one family's Christmases across generations."

He sounds wistful almost, and the urge to be nosy rises in me. I want to know more about him. I know he has a mom and stepmom. Does he know his biological father? Does he have siblings or aunts and uncles? Grandparents? Why doesn't he have a Christmas tree if he wants one?

But I can hear my family moving around and heading closer to the front door. If we want a decent spot to see the parade, we need to go. "Everybody's heading out. We walk, but I know Dad's boots aren't a perfect fit. We can take the Jeep if you want, and I'll park at the fire station."

"Walking sounds good. Should I unplug this while we're gone?" I nod and he pulls the plug on the lights.

By the time he gets his boots and coat on, the rest of the family has gone ahead. We take our time, since I know my parents will find a good spot and we'll just squeeze in with them.

"You all don't ride on the floats?" he asks. "Isn't that a thing people do?"

"We used to. Once Mel got old enough to watch the parade, though, my parents thought that would be more fun. Erin will be on the library's float and Rob—my brother—will be driving the fire truck. But the school chorus will be on the Charming Inn float, and it'll stop a few times so the kids can sing for the crowd."

"Good advertising," he says, sounding impressed.

We join my parents in time for the start of the parade. My dad hoists Elsie onto his shoulders so she can see, so of course Mel talks Donovan into lifting her onto his. She's bigger than her sister, but the weight doesn't seem to bother him.

When the fire truck goes by, my brother does a double take at the sight of his wildly waving niece sitting on the shoulders of a man he doesn't know, and then he frowns at me. I smile back at Rob, and he can see the rest of the family doesn't seem to have a problem with the situation. I know he'll be calling my mom the second he parks that truck, though.

After the parade, my family starts discussing which booths they want to hit first. They also want to plan their route around snacks. We have the same conversation and we follow the same path around town every year.

This year, I have other plans.

"Donovan and I are going to go wander," I tell my parents. When my dad opens his mouth to protest, my mom steps on his foot and I hope Donovan didn't notice.

Then we're finally alone to explore the magic of the Charming Lake Christmas fair. Since we all know each other in this town, we'd all decided over breakfast we'd introduce Donovan as the son of my dad's college roommate. Personally, I thought *friend from out of town visiting* would have sufficed, but Mom said people would wonder how any of us had made out-of-town friends, so it was easier to go with their story. Maybe she was right, because everybody seemed to accept the introduction without raising any eyebrows.

"You're surprisingly good at navigating my family's

nonsense," I say after introducing him for what felt like the fiftieth time.

"Pivoting and going with the flow is part of what I do. And this is a lot more enjoyable." He holds up the cup he's been sipping from. "Plus, there's hot chocolate with candy canes in it. I had no idea I was missing out."

"Wait until you get one of Mrs. Johnson's snickerdoodles. They make you feel so good, Jace actually had them tested for drugs three years ago." When he stops walking to look at me, I laugh. "They were clean. They're just *that* good, apparently."

Before we get to the Santa Fund's bake sale, where Mrs. Johnson's snickerdoodles reign supreme, though, we pass by the small park where Santa's holding court in the massive wooden sleigh.

"You should sit in the sleigh and tell Santa what you want for Christmas," I say, and I'm rewarded with that stern frown I find a little sexy.

"Why would I do that?"

"Because it's a fun tradition and I get the feeling you could use more fun in your life."

He snorts. "Now you sound like my mother."

And there's my in. "I bet getting a picture of you with Santa would not only prove to your mom you can have fun, but it would cheer her up."

"It's ridiculous."

"That's why she'll love it." Even though he's shaking his head, I can tell he's considering it. "It'll make her laugh."

"You're right."

I take his hand to pull him into the line, and he doesn't let it go. The feel of our fingers locked together thrills me, and I don't even care that a lot of my neighbors will notice and probably be talking about it for weeks to come.

Let them talk.

When it's our turn, he looks like he's going to back out, but I release his hand and give him a little push. He's a good sport about it and when I hold my phone up to take the picture, he leans close to the town's Santa and gives me a grin that's entirely too naughty considering the situation.

"Get in with him and I'll take your picture," I hear Lyla say.

I hadn't realized she was nearby and I turn to her, about to laugh off her comment. I don't need my entire family getting ideas in their head about Donovan and me. I have plenty of ideas of my own.

"Come on, Natalie," Donovan calls. "Come tell me and Santa what you want for Christmas."

I can't say no to him. I hand Lyla my phone and climb into the sleigh. Then I awkwardly climb over Donovan's lap to sit between him and Santa. Donovan puts his arm around me, pulling me close, and our gazes lock.

"I asked Santa for more of that hot cocoa," he whispers, and we both laugh.

"Got it," Lyla calls.

"We hadn't even looked at the camera yet," I say, and she holds up the phone even though I can't see the picture from the sleigh.

"It's perfect," she insists.

I want to argue, but the Dillon twins are jumping up and down, unable to contain their excitement at being next to talk to Santa. Donovan climbs down first so he can help me. I expect him to take my hands just for balance, but he wraps his hands around my waist and lifts me off the sleigh. Instinctively, I put my hands on his shoulders to steady myself.

My feet hit the ground without me breaking eye contact with him, which means I'm looking up. We're definitely in kissing range. Just a little stretch up onto my toes and our mouths would touch.

One of the Dillon twins bumps me in his rush to get to the sleigh and the spell is broken.

When I turn to retrieve my phone, Lyla's looking at me in a way that suggests I'm going to have to explain what's going on between me and Donovan in the very near future.

She hands me my phone. "Mom says Erin needs the rest of the popcorn at the library and I promised the girls I'd take them through the candy cane maze."

"I'll get it. Thanks for this."

After she's gone, I pull up the pictures on my phone. The one of Donovan and Santa is just as fun as I'd hoped, but the one Lyla took of the two of us takes my breath away.

We look like we're—

"Can you send that to my mom, since her number's in your phone?" Donovan asks, yanking me away from thoughts that are only going to get me in trouble. "And to my phone, too? I don't have it right now, but hopefully I'll see it again someday."

I hand him my phone and watch as he types his number into my contacts. He sends both pictures to himself, and then he types a message to his mom and attaches them. I hear the whooshing sound, and then he mutters a curse.

"I didn't mean to send her both," he says, and it's clear he's mostly talking to himself.

I'm not sure if he wants to hide the fact he's stuck in Charming Lake with a woman whose company he's enjoying or if he's afraid his mom will join my mom in trying to play amateur matchmaker. Either way, I pretend I didn't hear him.

He hands my phone back to me. "I'm ready for one of those allegedly unnaturally good snickerdoodles, I think."

CHAPTER *Twelve*

Donovan

I'M NOT surprised when the flip-phone in my pocket buzzes not even two minutes after I sent the text to my mother from Natalie's phone.

I hadn't meant to send both photos. I hadn't been thinking straight because the photo Lyla took of Natalie and me had knocked the wind out of me. It was like an image of a life I could never have, but that I'm starting to think I really want.

And my mother is going to see that. Instead of saying I'd stayed with a nice family who owned an inn and leaving it at that—nursing my regret about what could have been privately—I was going to have to explain Natalie and our almost instant connection to her.

Well, instant *not* counting the meeting at the airport, of course. I hadn't been at my best at that moment.

"I have to go back to the inn and grab the rest of the popcorn," Natalie says just as my phone buzzes a second time. "It's in a bag, which is light, so you go ahead and get your snickerdoodle and I'll meet you there."

"Don't you want help?"

"It's popcorn. I've got this."

I want to go with her, but I also want to find a reasonably quiet spot to call my mom. I'm afraid if I don't respond to the text messages she's sending to the flip-phone, she'll resort to texting Natalie's phone. That could be an embarrassing disaster.

"Keep walking that way and you'll find the Santa Fund bake sale on the left." Then she's gone before I can say anything else.

Instead of heading straight for the cookies, I walk between two buildings to find the closest thing to privacy I can get in the middle of a Christmas fair. Mom answers on the first ring, so I know she still had her phone in her hand.

"Donovan?"

"Hi, Mom."

"Who is that woman? Where are you?"

"Her name's Natalie. She was the one giving me a ride to Stowe when the weather turned, and she runs the inn for her family. The town's having their Christmas fair, and they lured me here with the promise of snickerdoodles."

"I see the promise of a lot more than cookies in that picture."

I pinch the bridge of my nose and sigh. "Don't, Mom."

"But—"

"I'll tell you all about it when we get home. But I need you to promise when you and Judy pick me up on Sunday

—tomorrow—that you don't say anything to embarrass me. They're nice people. I cracked a joke and we were laughing. That's all."

"Fine. Go stuff yourself with snickerdoodles, and you can tell me about it on the plane."

"Love you."

I slide the phone back into my pocket and lean against the clapboard siding for a moment. *Tomorrow.* I'm leaving tomorrow, so by tomorrow night, Natalie Byrne won't be a part of my life anymore. And no matter what her motivation was for inviting me in, I know my life is going to feel pretty empty for a while.

Snickerdoodles are a great way to lift the spirits, so I walk back to the sidewalk and start making my way in the direction Natalie had pointed. I take my time, stopping at booths and displays along the way.

I come to a folding card table that has a framed photo of a woman and a little girl next to a big glass fishbowl that's filling up with coins and crumpled bills.

"Hello, stranger and happy holidays," the older woman in a bright purple coat behind the table says. "We're raising money to buy a van for Mandy Reynolds and her little girl, Amelia."

I look at the big plywood sign she points to and note the goal number at the top. One hundred thousand dollars. The red paint tracking their progress rises to the twenty-eight thousand mark, which is pretty impressive for small town fundraising.

One hundred thousand dollars.

The final piece of the puzzle that is Natalie clicks into place. The amazing and loving woman I've gotten to know hadn't seen a mercenary opportunity to fleece me out of a hundred grand. She'd seen an opportunity to get a van for

Amelia from a man who won't miss the money, rather than watching her community scrape it together over what would probably take years.

"Amelia has spina bifida, and it's getting hard for Mandy to lift her into her minivan. It would be cheaper to refit hers than to buy a whole new van, but that van's been on its last legs for at least two years now. It's a miracle it's still running, so it would be just her luck that she'd get it all set up with an expensive wheelchair lift and it would die on her."

"There are grants and foundations that can help."

"Sure. Erin, over at the library, helped Mandy apply for a bunch, but we can't sit around waiting to see if she gets any help. We'll keep raising money and if a grant comes through, we'll put the money we raise toward her medical bills. Mandy was struggling even before her no-good husband took off. It was all too much for him, he said."

I don't say anything for a few seconds. I'm too busy swallowing the rage I feel toward a man I've never met so I can open my mouth without a string of expletives erupting.

Once I'm in control again, I look at the photo of the little girl. "I don't have my checkbook with me. Can you write down a name and address where I can send a donation?"

"Sure can." The woman digs around in her purse until she finds a pen and a receipt to write on the back of. "She has an account at the bank just for the fundraising because the news did a story and it's the safest way for direct donations. And there's a GoFundMe, so I'll write that info down for you, too."

"I appreciate it. And I'll definitely be sending a donation as soon as I can arrange it."

"Thank you. And Merry Christmas."

I figure out how to use the flip-phone to take a photo of the information she wrote on the receipt before tucking it into my pocket. Then I turn around and walk back the way we came.

CHAPTER
Thirteen

Natalie

"THE HUNDRED THOUSAND dollars is for Amelia's van, isn't it?"

I spin, almost dropping the last box of the Christmas popcorn I'd been sent to fetch. I didn't hear him come in. "Don't scare people holding food for the Christmas fair, Donovan. And yes, it is."

"Why didn't you tell me?"

I shrug, not sure I can make him understand. "Does it really matter?"

"I've spent the last couple of days trying to reconcile the woman who wanted a hundred grand to help a stranger during the holidays with...you. You're all about family, friends, and community, and I don't think you have a mercenary bone in your body. So maybe it *doesn't* really matter, but I'd like to know."

"I thought you were saying whatever you had to so I'd

give you a ride, but then you'd blow me off." I set the bag on the counter since we'll probably be here a few minutes. "And that would have sucked, but also been expected. But if I told you about Mandy and Amelia—and why I wanted that amount—and you blew me off, it would feel more personal, maybe. I'd be angry and hate you, and I like to avoid negativity whenever I can."

"And you didn't tell anybody else about the money. Is that also because you thought I'd blow you off?"

"Yes. I would have been disappointed and angry, but if they thought Mandy was getting her van and then didn't, they would have been heartbroken. I never want that, but especially not at Christmastime."

He's been moving toward me as I speak, and now he's close enough so I have to tip my head back slightly to look him in the eye.

"Do you still think that?" His voice is low and his gaze locks on my face, as if he's sure he'll be able to tell if I'm lying. "Do you still think I'll blow you off?"

"No." Relief relaxes his features, which makes it easier for me to talk. "You're not the only one who's let go of first impressions."

"So I'm not an airport jerk?"

I laugh. "Oh, no. You were totally a jerk in the airport and I assumed you were a guy with a suit and too much money who thought the world served him. But I've learned that when you're not scared for your mom and unable to get to her, you're a pretty decent guy."

"Pretty decent, huh?" He chuckles and takes another step toward me. He was already close to start with, so our bodies are almost touching now. "It almost sounds like you like me."

My heart squeezes in my chest. Yes, I like him. I like

him a *lot* and I don't want him to know that. This is temporary—a holiday interlude—and I want to keep it fun and light. Amelia gets her van, Donovan gets to soak up some Christmas spirit, and I get to flirt with a billionaire. And we're leaving it there because he and I don't work in the real world.

"You're okay," I tease, and then his hand is in my hair, lifting my face to his.

There's nothing tentative about this kiss. His mouth is demanding, as if he's claiming me, and I part my lips for his tongue. His fingers tighten in my hair and I moan, my hands sliding under his coat so I can run my hands over his back. I've never hated flannel more than now, when it's a barrier between my palms and his naked skin.

He catches my bottom lip between his teeth and pauses, the muscles in his back taut as his quick breaths match mine. Then my lower back is against the island, his hips pressed to mine as my fingernails dig into the flannel.

I'm trying to calculate how long we have before somebody comes looking for me—and the popcorn—when the doorbell rings, a resounding chime that startles me because nobody ever rings the doorbell. I didn't even realize it still works.

"Saved by the bell," Donovan mutters as I pull away, his hand sliding free of my hair.

Honestly, I'd rather ignore the bell and drag Donovan upstairs or into the coat closet or anywhere even remotely semi-private, but I can't. Whoever's standing on the porch is obviously a stranger and here for a reason.

And when I open the door and see a young guy in jeans and a sports hoodie holding an outrageously expensive-looking leather briefcase, I know what the reason is.

Donovan's *real* life has shown up at the inn, and the party's over.

I invite the young man in, and I watch as Donovan opens the briefcase. I spot a slim wallet and a smartphone inside, along with a lot of papers and folders, and then he closes and locks it again. He has to sign for it, and then the guy leaves.

"I guess that's the end of your holiday fun, huh?" I have no doubt he's going to lock himself away to catch up on email and stocks and whatever else it is super rich people do all day.

He looks at me for a long time, and I can't tell what he's thinking. Then he picks up the briefcase. "Wait here."

I watch him go up the stairs and then I follow the sound of his footsteps in the hall. I hear his door close and then the footsteps retrace the path back to the stairs. He doesn't have the case with him, and I realize he must have just tossed it into his room.

He meets me at the bottom of the stairs and gives me a smile that melts my heart. "Let's go deliver that popcorn so I can get my snickerdoodle."

CHAPTER Fourteen

Donovan

CONSIDERING how much walking I've done today and the amount of festivity I've taken part in, I should be exhausted. Every time I lock eyes with Natalie, though, it's like getting a shot of pure adrenaline.

Being with her gives me the kind of rush I usually only get from coming out on top in a tense negotiation or bringing an allegedly impossible development deal together.

Maybe that's why the very first emotion I felt when I saw my briefcase was regret. Not relief or a need to touch base with my email or spreadsheets, but regret that the forced festivity is coming to an end.

And maybe that rush I feel when Natalie looks at me is why, despite having multiple businesses to run and my right-hand woman being unavailable, I tossed my recovered briefcase on the bed and haven't looked back.

I don't want this weekend to end.

Plus, there's knowing now that she's not a woman who was looking to take advantage of a stranger in need. Reminding myself of that misconception had been the brakes I employed every time my imagination started running away with my common sense.

Now I have no brakes, and my imagination is a runaway train as I sit on a hay bale next to Natalie. We're sipping hot cocoa and watching the revelry going on around us, and she's close enough so the length of her thigh is warm against mine.

"Did you have fun today?" she asks.

I should lie to her—and to myself—and tell her I'd rather have been catching up on work instead, but I can't make myself say the words. "I did. A lot of fun, actually."

"See? There *is* more to life than business. And maybe when you get out of here and get back to your laptop and your shiny office, you'll see that it didn't all crumble because you spent a couple of days off the grid, eating Christmas cookies and driving in the snow."

I can feel the words rising in my throat and I try to stop them. I've never told any woman why I'm so driven—why succeeding at business is not only something I'm good at, but necessary if I want to take an easy breath. Hustling and pushing all day is the only way I can relax enough to sleep at night.

But she's looking at me with her eyes sparkling and her cheeks red from the cold, and the words spill out.

"My dad died because we were poor and had no health insurance, and he couldn't afford to take time off or get medical care. By the time he ended up in the emergency room, it was too late. He was terminal, and he was gone two months later. I swore I wouldn't lose my mother that way."

"I'm so sorry," she says, clutching the sleeve of my borrowed coat. "So you just...became a billionaire?"

"It wasn't easy, and it wasn't fast. Also, I've only technically been a billionaire for about six months. Just a lot of millions before that." I remember, during that final climb, wondering if hitting the billion mark would finally set me free of the fear. It didn't. "I started with gambling. Small stuff because we were broke, but if I found a dollar, I could make it five. I mastered poker and sports betting while learning everything I could about the stock market. Then I gambled there and earned enough to gamble in real estate."

"That's a lot of gambling."

"I'm good at it. I didn't go to college or have connections to give me a hand up, but I can read people. I can calculate risk versus reward. And I can bluff my way through almost anything."

"Are you happy, though?"

I can't really wrap my head around what that means. I'm proud of the businesses I've built. I'm free of the fear my mom will go without medical care or have to choose between groceries or heat.

"What would happen if you stepped back?"

I look at her, and the compassion I see in her dark eyes is like a punch to my chest. "What do you mean?"

"Would you be poor again?"

"No. I'd have to work really hard at *losing* money to ever be poor again. I give away a lot, actually, but what's left keeps generating more." I blow out a long, slow breath. "But then I start dreaming about the day I yelled at my dad because he wasn't even trying to live, and he told me we didn't have the money to fight a battle he would lose, and he wouldn't leave us in debt. And then I wake up and work harder."

I can hear it when I say it out loud like that. I've never verbalized those fears before and the confession feels like that satisfying pop of a jar lid that's been a long struggle to open.

"Have you ever talked to somebody about it? Professionally, I mean?" she asks gently, and I shake my head. "I think a childhood trauma like that will always be a wound, but if it's affecting your ability to enjoy your life this many years later, it's an *open* wound, and it's okay to talk to a professional about it."

I nod because she's right, and also because I'm not sure I can speak right now. Luckily, Mel and Elsie run up to us with a visibly exhausted Lyla behind them.

"It's time!" Mel yells, and I don't know what she's talking about, but I'm grateful my conversation with Natalie has been put on pause.

Elsie puts her hands on her hips and glares at me. "Are you going to watch *Elf* with us?"

I can't tell if she wants me to say yes or no. "I don't know. I've never seen it."

All four of them gasp, and Natalie puts her hand on my arm. "You've never seen *Elf*?"

"Nope."

Mel shakes her head sadly, but then she rallies and bounces on her toes while clapping her hands. "You have to watch it with us. We eat baked macaroni and cheese and watch *Elf* after the parade. It's a family tradition."

Her excitement is infectious, but I can't resist teasing her. "I don't want to barge in on a family tradition, though."

"Oh, you're watching *Elf* with us," Natalie says, standing and then pulling me to my feet.

"You should warn him about the baked mac," I hear Lyla mutter to her sister, and we're all laughing as we walk back to the inn.

And taking Natalie's hand in mine feels like the most natural thing in the world.

CHAPTER
Fifteen

Natalie

THE FIRST THING I see when Donovan opens his door is the naked wall of his chest and I forget the words I'd rehearsed on the way down the hall.

My gaze flicks downward, but the nakedness doesn't continue below the waist. He's wearing sweatpants and his feet are bare. I can tell by the lingering smell of soap and the dampness in his hair that he took a shower after the movie.

He backs up, giving me space to enter. I don't want space. I want to rub up against him on the way by, but I don't. I try to come up with something to say as he closes the door behind me, and I fall back on pretending I'm here as the host.

"I saw your light was on and wanted to make sure you have everything you need before I go upstairs."

The corners of his mouth twitch as if he's barely

keeping a straight face. "The service here really *is* five-star."

"I aim to please." Crap, why did my voice get so low and husky all of a sudden? That came out a lot more suggestive than I intended.

Or maybe I *had* intended it to be suggestive because what I really wanted to say was *hey, you're leaving tomorrow and I'm never going to see you again, but how about we get naked and make a memory that'll keep me warm for a long time?*

But I don't have to say anything else because he's moving toward me. He cups his hand behind my neck and I have a few seconds to run my hand over his naked chest before his mouth is on mine.

The kiss is hot and deep. His tongue slides between my lips, dancing with mine, while his other hand cups my breast. I'm not wearing a bra, and when he runs his thumb over the taut nipple, the sensation is like a zap through my body.

I run my hands down his back until they reach the sweatpants. Then I tuck my fingers under the waistband, my nails running over his lower back.

But when I slide them toward the front of the waist-band, he breaks off the kiss and grabs my wrists. "Wait."

Wait? Did he really just ask me to wait? But I take a step back, giving him a little space.

"Do you have…I don't tuck condoms in my suit coat pockets when I go to business meetings."

"Oh." Relief rushes through me. "I brought one with me, just in case."

His forehead rests against mine. "That's a relief. This seems like the kind of town where a man smashing a store window to get a box of condoms would be talked about for a very long time."

"At least they wouldn't be able to ID you," I tease, pulling the condom from the pocket of my shorts and tossing it on the nightstand.

Forty-five seconds later, I'm naked. The haste with which he peels my sleep shirt off makes me worry he's going to rush things. Sure, I'm starving for his touch, but I also hope we're not going to burn through both condoms in ten minutes or less.

But once our clothes are strewn around our feet, he takes a deep breath and runs his hands over my shoulders and down my arms. Then he slides them around my waist and hauls me against him. I gasp as our naked bodies finally come together, and he kisses me. His mouth is demanding and when he buries his hand in my hair, I moan.

He kisses me until I can barely breathe and I certainly don't remember my own name. All I know is that his mouth feels good and his hands feel good, and I want more of him. *All* of him.

I'm not sure how we make it to the bed without falling since we don't take our hands off each other. He's definitely in charge, pinning my hands to the mattress as he licks and sucks almost every part of my body until I'm whimpering his name and begging for him.

I hear the crinkle of the condom wrapper, and then he's between my thighs. He looks down at me, our gazes locking. I reach up and stroke his face. I can't help myself.

He turns his head and captures my index finger between his lips. Then he takes it in his mouth and sucks hard. I rake my fingernails up his back and his muscles tremble under my touch.

Then he reaches down and guides his erection into me. Each thrust takes him deeper until his length fills me. I whisper his name, my fingers tangled in his hair, as he starts to move.

Time ceases to exist. There's only Donovan and the heat that the sweet friction is sending through my body. I stroke his back and run my hands over his ass, and he kisses me. He kisses my jaw. My neck. He sucks one nipple and then the other, capturing it between his teeth with just enough pressure to make me whimper.

Then his pace quickens, each thrust coming harder and faster. I know he's close and I reach down to stroke my clit while my other hand grasps his hip, urging him on.

The orgasm takes my breath away, and as my back arches off the bed, I have to bite down on my lip to keep from moaning his name. I'm still trembling, waiting to breathe again, when his body jerks and he comes with a groan. I run my hands over his back as his hips pulse before he collapses on top of me.

He kisses the side of my neck, his hand cupping my breast, and I close my eyes to savor the delicious post-orgasm glow. He finally lifts his head enough to give me a deep kiss, and then he pushes off of me. One more kiss, this time on the tip of my breast, and he disappears into the bathroom.

When he comes back, he hauls me into his arms and makes a *mmm* sound close to my ear. Locked in his embrace, I close my eyes and savor the feeling of being held. I can feel his heartbeat as it slows against my cheek, and his breathing follows suit as he drifts toward sleep.

I don't drift into sleep, though. Once he's fully asleep, his muscles relax, and I know I can probably get out of bed without waking him.

It's tempting to stay. I want to fall asleep curled against his body. I want to wake up to warm, sleepy kisses.

But he's leaving tomorrow. This was all I get of him and the longer I stay in this bed, pretending otherwise, the harder it's going to be to watch him leave.

Slowly and silently, I slide from the bed and gather my clothes. I pull them on because it would be just my luck I'd run into somebody heading to the kitchen for a midnight snack.

Then, after allowing myself a last look at his face—so relaxed in sleep—I sneak out of his room and back to my own.

CHAPTER Sixteen

Donovan

I WAKE UP ALONE.

I don't like entanglements and distractions, so there have been very few mornings in my adult life I *haven't* woken up alone, but it hits differently today. All I want to do right now is roll over and bury my face in Natalie's hair while my hand skims up her naked side to cup her breast.

But she's not here and that line of thought is only going to make this morning more painful—emotionally *and* physically—so I take a fast and freezing shower before dressing in the suit I was wearing the day I got here. Stella had thrown the shirt and undergarments in the wash for me the day after I arrived, and I steamed the coat and pants in the shower. I don't look my best, but I'm a little more myself.

I'm not sure what to do with the clothing I've worn. I'd been tossing it in the basket each night, but I hate leaving dirty laundry. It would feel strange to haul it on a private plane in a garbage bag, though. I decide to leave it, knowing they'll wash it when they do the bedding, and probably put it back in the attic.

I realize I slept in a lot later than usual, so there's nobody in the dining room. I'm not sure there's anybody in the house at all, but then I walk into the kitchen and find Natalie sitting at the island.

She smiles when she sees me, her cheeks flushing slightly. "Good morning, sleepyhead."

"Good morning." I go straight to the coffeepot. "Did I actually sleep through Mel and Elsie getting up?"

"You did. I was giving you another ten minutes or so and then I was going to do a wellness check."

I sit at the island and sip the coffee, trying to wake up. I don't know exactly what time Mom and Judy will be here, but I know when their chartered flight is scheduled to leave Manchester, so I know they'll be here sooner than I'd like.

I hadn't meant to sleep away so much of the little time I have left with Natalie.

"Where is everybody?" I ask because I really don't hear anybody else in the house.

"My parents are out in the barn, breaking down the float. And Lyla had to bring the girls to her former mother-in-law's house for their visitation. Then she was going to go help Erin break down the library float. Using books sounds like a good idea until you have to put them all back."

We're essentially alone, but she's given no indication I should put down my coffee cup and kiss her instead. She hasn't even moved her stool closer to mine.

"I see you're back in the suit," she says, and I don't

think I'm imagining the hint of sadness in her voice. "You must be eager to get back to your regularly scheduled life."

I shake my head because she's wrong about that. I'm not eager to get back to my regular life. It's too hard to imagine what it will look like without Natalie in it, and it hurts to try.

I don't want to go.

Actually, it's not the going—I'm ready to get back to the city. It's having to leave Natalie that's the problem. I'm not ready to leave her behind.

"Come with me." I don't mean to say the words out loud, but I don't regret them.

For a few seconds, my mind offers up images of Natalie throwing herself into my arms. Her in my penthouse apartment. Her naked in front of the Christmas tree she talks me into buying and decorating last minute.

She doesn't throw herself into my arms, though. She frowns. "To the airport?"

"What?"

"You want me to go with you to the airport?"

"No." It takes my brain a few seconds to catch up. "I mean, I want you to come to the airport with me, yes. And then I want you to get on the plane with me. I want you to come home with me for the holidays."

Her eyes widen as her breath catches, and the way her face lights up tells me I must have been a very good boy this year because I'm about to get the only thing I want for Christmas.

Then the light dims as she takes a deep breath. "Donovan, I…"

I don't want her to finish that sentence, but I can't

speak. I can feel years of conditioning straightening my spine and controlling my expression, and I can't stop it.

"I can't just leave," she says.

I should cup her face, look her in the eye, and beg. I don't. "You said the inn's closed to guests right now."

"It is, but it's Christmas. My family has plans, and I promised my nieces we'd..." She stops, pressing her lips together for a few seconds. "You can stay here."

"I can't do that." The statement is a reflex, but it's true. While I have great senior staff, Annette and I both going off-grid for days could have set a dozen fires I need to put out.

"I'm pretty sure a guy like you can do whatever you want. So it's not that you can't—it's that you *won't*."

In the silence that follows, while I try to think of something—anything—I can say to salvage the conversation, I hear the crunch of tires on the driveway.

"That's not Lyla," Natalie says, getting up to walk to the window. "It's a big, black SUV, so I assume it's for you."

I know Mom and Judy like to get on the road early when they're traveling, but their timing today couldn't be worse.

"Natalie," I say, standing and taking a step toward her.

"Don't make this harder," she says, and my stomach knots. "We had fun, Donovan. We made some memories, and now it's time to go back to our lives. Now, go greet your mom and her wife, and I'll make you another coffee in a to-go cup."

A to-go cup. Just like that. *Here's your coffee and there's the door.*

I'm on the front porch when the driver opens my mother's door and helps her out of the SUV. She smiles when she sees me, but whatever she sees on my face sobers her. She waits for Judy and then they walk up the steps together, with Mom slightly leaning on her for support because of the plastic boot she's wearing.

"It's fine. I'll follow up with my doctor when I get home, but it's nothing to worry about," Mom says after I kiss each of them on the cheek. "How are *you* doing?"

"I'm fine, thanks to the Byrnes' hospitality."

"Welcome to the Charming Inn," Natalie says from behind me, and my body tenses. "Please come in and I'll show you where you can freshen up if you'd like. And we have some leftover goodies from the Christmas fair, so I packed some into a basket."

Watching my mom interact with Natalie as she gets a brief tour of the historic inn, I can see that they'd get along really well. But Mom is taking her cues from me and isn't as warm and open as she usually is.

I'm not ready when I find myself at the door with a coffee in one hand and my briefcase in the other. Natalie hands Judy a small wicker basket with pastries and other snacks tucked under a cloth.

"I put a few snickerdoodles in there," Natalie tells me, and I can see the effort it's taking her to smile at me.

"Thank you." I clear my throat, but it doesn't seem to clear the lump of emotion making my voice hoarse. "Natalie, I—"

"We should go if we want to have time to stop at that yarn store you read about," Judy says, oblivious to the vibe in the room as usual.

"Safe travels," Natalie says, taking a step back. "It was a pleasure to meet you all."

I don't want to go.

But somehow I'm swept up by Mom and Judy, and

before I quite realize what's happening, I'm in the front passenger seat of a hired SUV. I'm reaching for the door handle—I can't leave like this—when the driver puts it in gear, which triggers the door locks.

Then we're moving and as the driver takes the turn onto the main road, I get a glimpse of Natalie still standing on the porch with her hand pressed to her mouth, watching us leave.

And then she's gone.

CHAPTER Seventeen

Natalie

MONDAY'S A NIGHTMARE. With the fun of the fair behind us, the sugar high over, and Christmas in one week, there's a frantic energy in Charming Lake I find stressful. I love the holidays, but the panic that sets in toward the end isn't my favorite.

And I'm nursing a broken heart after a sleepless night, so I'm not at my best. I'm pretty sure that's why Mom has me out running her errands. The tape she forgot to buy. Mailing the cards she always means to send out the day after Thanksgiving and never does.

And I don't even stop at the general store for coffee because it just reminds me of Donovan. With everything crossed off the list Mom gave me, I'm ready to go home, claim a headache, and hide in my room for a while.

But I glance at the fundraising progress board as I do

every time I drive by, and then I stop, right there in the road.

The red paint goes all the way up to the top now. One hundred thousand dollars raised. Tears spring to my eyes and I squeeze the steering wheel to keep from crying. Then I see somebody propped a second board against a tree next to the first, and I lose the battle. The tears stream down my cheeks when I see a line of red paint leading to *$300,000* with an exclamation point.

Donovan.

My billionaire stray has come through on his promise, and Mandy and Amelia—hell, the entire town of Charming Lake—will have a very happy Christmas this year. My holiday joy is dimmed, though, because Donovan didn't stay.

I sit there, tears streaming down my face, until the car behind me lays on the horn. Swiping at my cheeks, I give an apologetic wave to the rearview mirror and hit the gas. Messy emotions clog my head as I drive home, and I can't stop the slow trickle of tears.

Once I'm back at the inn, I sit in my car and scrub my face with the sleeves of my sweater. I don't want my family to see me cry. It's almost Christmas and I don't want anybody feeling as if they can't make merry around me. I also don't want them thinking I'm ridiculous. I get that I just met the man. And I can't explain to them it doesn't matter how long I've known him—what I felt for Donovan was potent and it was real.

I guess I don't do a good job of hiding the fact I've been crying because as soon as my mother sets eyes on me, she drags me into the kitchen. I don't think leaving Mel and Elsie alone with markers is a good idea, but she says they're washable. I never trust that label.

"What's going on?" she asks once we're in the kitchen.

I think about lying to her. I could tell her they were happy tears because Amelia is getting her van. Or I could say I'm just overwhelmed by all the things I have to do. But I can't look her in the eye and hide the truth.

"I miss Donovan."

"Oh, honey." She pats my hand, shaking her head. "He's a nice young man, and he clearly likes you. I think you'll hear from him again soon."

"I don't think so. And it wouldn't matter, anyway."

"Why not? If you think he's the one, you can't let him get away because of geography. It can be figured out."

"He's not just a guy who sells real estate in a nice suit, Mom. He's a freaking *billionaire*." I watch her eyes widen as that word sinks in. "He's super rich and a workaholic who spends all his time making even more money."

"A billionaire? Really?" Mom shakes her head. "Then you *definitely* shouldn't have let him get away."

"Why? So I can leave all of you and the inn and Charming Lake to go sit in a fancy apartment in the city alone, waiting for him to remember I'm there and put his phone down for five minutes?"

"He didn't seem like that at all. He had such a good time, and he was wonderful with the girls. You looked very happy together."

"We *were* happy together, but that wasn't the real him, Mom. He left his stuff on the plane and I brought him here and it was like a forced time out. He wouldn't have *chosen* to relax and go to the Christmas fair and watch *Elf*."

She thinks about it for a few seconds and then shakes her head. "No, but he did those things and truly had a good time. So maybe now he *would* choose those things."

Maybe he'd choose you, *Natalie* is what I hear. I won't tell her about his dad and how he's driven to work harder and make more money out of fear. And without that explanation, I can't make her understand that he's not free to actually make that choice. He won't be able to stop himself from putting business ahead of me.

Plus, I just don't want to talk about Donovan with my mother anymore.

I had the gift of a lovely weekend, as well as one magical night in his bed, and I just want to hold the memories—as painful as they are right now—close to my heart. I don't want to pick them apart and hope for more. There is no more.

But as I scrape dishes and load the dishwasher, I can't stop thinking about him being beside me. The way I'd teased him about knowing how to do chores, not knowing yet about his childhood and how it had forged the man he is now.

I should call him. I need to acknowledge he'd come through on his end of the bargain. That was a lot of money, and I should thank him for the donation personally.

Can I hear his voice without losing it, though? I'm not sure, and the last thing I want to do is call him and burst into tears. It would be embarrassing, plus I don't want to make him feel bad. There were no promises made.

Maybe I'll call him tomorrow. The conversation with my mother has me feeling raw, and I can't trust myself not to get emotional when I hear Donovan's voice. Tomorrow, or maybe the next day. I'll focus on getting ready for Christmas and I'll spend as much time as I can with Mel and Elsie, taking in their joy.

When I'm feeling steady enough, I'll call him and thank him for his donation. I'll ask after his mother and wish them a merry Christmas.

And then I'll hang up and spend a very long time missing him.

CHAPTER Eighteen

Donovan

I SHOULD BE CONTENT. I'm sitting behind the sleek mahogany desk in my home office suite. There's no clutter, but the room walks a fine line between spartan and stark. Warm colors, wood and some tasteful art save it from being too austere, I think. The room is my command center, but it's also my refuge.

Not today, though. The silence is oppressive, rather than calming. The sense of control feels like a void where the Byrnes' chaos should be. And there aren't enough reports, spreadsheets, or graphs in the world to distract me from thoughts of Natalie. That's new. I've never had a woman take my whole attention away from business before, so I have no coping skills for it.

I want to call her. The need to hear her voice is so strong, it's almost a physical ache, and I've even picked up my phone several times. It wouldn't be out of line to call and let her know I made it home and thank her again for her hospitality and that of her family.

But then what?

A chime sounds, letting me know the elevator's on its way up. Since Annette isn't back yet, it must be my mother. I close the laptop I've barely looked at and meet her in the living room.

She kisses my cheek and then drops onto the leather sofa. "Am I interrupting anything that's *not* work?"

"No. I didn't know you'd be dropping by." I sit next to her, worry buzzing in my head. Mom's here a lot, but rarely does she arrive unexpectedly.

"I hadn't planned to. But then I pulled up the photos on my phone looking for a picture I took of my Christmas list and this came up."

She turns her phone to face me and the breath leaves my body in a rush when I see the picture of Natalie and me in the sleigh. With my arm around her and both of us laughing as we look at each other instead of the camera, we look like a happy couple, madly in love.

My heart aches and I rub my fingertips over my chest as if I can ease the pain. And my mother doesn't miss it.

"Why aren't you with her right now, Donovan?"

I wave my hand toward the office. "You know why."

"What does any of this matter compared to *this*?" She pushes the phone closer, as if the image isn't already seared into my soul. "Look how happy you are in this picture, Donovan. I've never seen you like this and, let me tell you, getting this text was one of the happiest moments of my life. I want this for you."

"And I want you to have the best of everything. I don't want you to ever go without something you need, and I don't care if it's doctors or a purse that catches your eye. You deserve *everything,* and that comes first. Always."

"There's no amount of money that can guarantee me health or happiness, Donovan."

"But I can make sure a *lack* of money doesn't stand in the way."

She sighs, and the sorrow in her eyes takes my breath away. "Your father didn't have the money to get the medical care he needed. That's a truth we'll always live with. But you need to remember what he *did* have. He had me. He had you. He had a family who loved him, and he had bedtime reading and teaching you to fish—or trying to, anyway—and watching the Red Sox games with you. His life wasn't nearly long enough, but it was a *good* and full life, well lived. That's what he would want for you."

"He would want me to take care of you."

"Honey, he would be so proud of what you've built. But he'd also be a little sad because it's *all* you have." She covers my hand with hers, but it doesn't take the sting out of her words. "Parents want their children to be happy and I don't think you are, and that hurts me. I won't say there's a void in my life. You don't have to have a wife and children for my life to be complete. But I don't think you're alone because that's the path you've chosen as your best life. It's more like you stepped into a gerbil wheel years ago and you're afraid to get out."

"If I get out, the wheel stops."

"Or somebody else—like Annette—steps in and keeps it going. And maybe it won't spin as fast or as hard without you in it, but…honey, does it really *have* to?"

I don't want to tell her about the dreams—about how I wake up in a cold sweat that drives me to the office to do *more.* To work harder and smarter.

"Donovan, you've set aside so much money in my accounts that you could lose everything tomorrow and I will still have more than I need. It's time—past time, honestly—for you to stop and think about what *you* want."

"Natalie." Her name leaves my lips before I can stop it, and my mom squeezes my hand.

Tears shimmer in her eyes, and her smile is warm and full of love. "It's time to let your heart lead for a while. And now I'm going to leave because I've said what I needed to say. And don't take this the wrong way, but I really hope we *don't* see you for Christmas dinner this year."

When the door closes behind my mother, I lean back and close my eyes. Instantly, I see Natalie's face, as I have every time I've closed my eyes since leaving her. I don't know if we can make it work. I don't know what our life together would look like. But I know I want to wake up next to her every morning forever, if she'll have me.

I have to try.

CHAPTER
Nineteen

Natalie

"HOW MANY MORE SLEEPS UNTIL Santa comes?" Elsie is tugging on the hem of my sweater as she asks, and I'm pretty sure it's the fourth time she's asked today.

"Two more sleeps. Tomorrow is Christmas Eve."

I'd tell her to check the advent calendar, but my dad got a craving in the middle of the night and opened all the doors so he could eat the chocolates. It's not the first year he's done it, either, so I'm not sure why we keep trying.

"Auntie Nat, Mister…*that man* is back!"

I freeze, my pulse racing as I try to remember how breathing works. It can't be. Donovan's gone back to his life and I stayed here in mine. He didn't even take my call this morning when I finally worked up the nerve to call the number he'd added to my contacts. It had gone to voicemail, and I'd left a painfully awkward message thanking him for his donation.

But it had to be Donovan. That's what Mel had called him.

And then I hear his voice. Mel laughing. The sound of Elsie abandoning me and running out to greet him.

I can't move. Donovan is back, and I don't know what it means. I'm afraid to hope, but I can't help myself and I'm still standing in the middle of the kitchen when he appears in the doorway.

"Merry almost Christmas," he says, and I make a weird gasping and sobbing and laughing sound.

"What's going on?" my mother is asking as she walks in from the dining room, and then she stops when she sees Donovan. She looks back and forth between us a few times, and then gestures for Mel and Elsie to come to her. "Girls, I need you to help me with…something. Let's go, um…somewhere else."

When we're alone again, I move toward Donovan and he moves toward me until we meet in the middle and his arms are around me. I'm trembling and I know he can feel it as he holds me tight with his cheek pressed to my hair.

"I've missed you so much," he says in a rough voice, and I'm glad his very expensive sweater is absorbing my tears. "I know it's only been a few days, but they were *very* long days."

"You came back," I manage to whisper.

"I couldn't shake the Ghost of Christmas in Charming Lake, I guess."

He pulls back when a door slams. I hear my mom talking, but I can't make out the low, urgent words. Then there's a lot of banging and the girls complaining they don't want to play in the snow. More urgent voices. Then the door slams again and the house is quiet. The yard's not, and it wouldn't surprise me to see my mother and sister's faces pressed against the window, but we're as close to alone as we can get.

I take Donovan's hand and lead him through the house to the sitting room. I don't want to stand in the kitchen while he tells me why he came back. We sit on the sofa and he turns slightly, so he's facing me.

"I don't have a lot of experience with being vulnerable," he says. "I swim with the sharks of the business world every day and any hint of weakness would make me the chum to their feeding frenzy. But this is different, and my feelings for you aren't a weakness—they make me stronger. Only if those feelings are mutual, of course, so I came here to find out, but I had no plan other than opening my mouth and hoping the right words fall out."

My heart is racing because I desperately want to know what *my feelings for you* means. I'm going to need him to be really specific about those feelings because the hope is becoming unmanageable.

"When you kidnapped me and took me out in the woods with your Jeep, you asked me if I was happy," he continues.

"Was it really a kidnapping, though? You were driving."

"I was coerced."

I laugh at him. "Coerced? How did I coerce you into being the driver in your own kidnapping?"

"I don't know, but you managed." He clears his throat. "Anyway, when you asked me if I was happy… I didn't know the answer to that question because I never really thought about it. It didn't matter. My mother was happy and healthy and that made me feel good because that's all I've wanted since the day my dad died."

I squeeze his hand, but I don't speak.

"When you called this morning, I didn't answer because I was in my first therapy session."

My breath catches in my chest, and I press my free hand to his cheek. "Donovan! That's wonderful."

"Yeah. I like her and I think she's going to help me overcome the fear that's been driving me." He smiles, giving a little shrug. "And then I listened to your voicemail and I wanted to call you back, but I already knew I was coming here. I was afraid if the conversation was awkward, I wouldn't come."

"I'm glad you're here. I missed you every second you were gone."

Our gazes lock, and I can feel just the hint of trembling in his hand. "I know we haven't known each other long, Natalie, but I'm falling in love with you. It's strong and it's real and I want to build a life together, no matter what it takes."

"I'm falling in love with you, too. And I want us to be together, whatever that looks like."

"When I say whatever it takes, I mean that. I'll live here in Charming Lake with you and work remotely and… maybe we can open a restaurant."

I laugh, pushing at his shoulder. "You can't open a restaurant just so you don't have to eat my mom's baked macaroni and cheese or have cereal for breakfast anymore."

"Actually, I can," he says with a chuckle. "*We* can. Or we can hire a chef. Or subscribe to a food delivery service. We can do whatever makes us both happy."

"Waking up with you on Christmas morning would make me happy."

"Me, too." He leans in and kisses me thoroughly. So thoroughly I'm breathless, half straddling his lap, and my hair is mussed by the time the kiss ends.

Then he grins. "My luggage is in the car. I brought my own underwear this time."

Epilogue

Donovan

Four years later…

"I REALLY NEED to get home for the Christmas parade," I tell the man whose car has died and is blocking my SUV in, as well as multiple other cars trying to get out.

"Oh, why didn't you say so?" the man says. "All of these other folks just thought a week before Christmas would be a good time to drive around in an airport parking garage, I guess."

Okay, I probably deserve the attitude. And I remember Natalie calling me out for being a jerk in this same airport four years ago. I take a deep breath and lower my voice.

"I apologize. I know it's a hectic time. It's just that my

wife is *very* pregnant and I promised her I'd be home today."

"That poor kid's going to get shafted on gifts," the man says, shaking his head as he stares at his car.

I can't believe I'm stuck in this airport again. At least this time I have my wallet and my phone. And the keys to my vehicle, even if I can't get it out of its parking spot right now. I drive myself whenever I can these days, rather than using a car service, but I regret that decision at the moment.

All I can do is wait while three men stick their heads under the open hood and try to figure out what's wrong with it. Throwing money at the car won't help and I've forgotten everything my dad taught me about engines, so I sit in the SUV rather than hover and glare.

When I put my phone in the holder, the contact makes the screen light up with a photo of Natalie and Sam. My wife looks beautiful sitting on the porch of the Charming Inn with our three-year-old son hugging her baby bump. My heart aches with the need to hold them and I'm about to go down to the first level and start trying to buy somebody's car when I hear an engine fire up.

The car isn't running great, but it's enough so it moves. I have to wait until the backup of waiting cars clears and then—finally—I'm on my way home.

They'll all be at the inn, making popcorn for tomorrow's Christmas fair, and completing the floats. My mom and Judy will be there, since they're family now, too. I don't stop at the house on the lake we bought and remodeled. I can't wait that long.

As I drive through the town, I slow so I can take in the glow of lights and let the feeling of peace and festivity really sink in. We have the home in New York City, where

Annette heads up the office, and in Florida and Colorado, but nothing beats the feeling of coming home to Charming Lake.

I'm not a billionaire anymore. After selling off the excess and dialing back to the core businesses, the companies are back to millions. But there's more than enough of those to provide livelihoods for everybody who depends on it, and I'm one hundred percent happier. The therapy helps, too. I've never canceled my weekly virtual sessions, and I feel stronger. Healthier and balanced.

And whole, thanks to the love of the woman who steps out onto the porch when I turn up the Charming Inn's long driveway.

Natalie looks radiant, and she laughs when I lift her into my arms. I kiss her, loving the feel of her round belly against me, and then set her gently on her feet.

"You made it," she says, holding my face in her hands.

"I told you I would." I had to wrap up a deal overseas and it couldn't be done remotely. I've been gone almost ten days, and it felt like forever. I was going to put it off until after the holidays, but leaving Natalie with a newborn would have been even harder. "You shouldn't be out here without a coat."

"This baby's like a furnace. I wanted the fresh air. And I wanted a chance to kiss you before Sam and the girls get hold of you. Justine is trying to teach the girls how to knit and—just so you know—the thing they're going to wrap around your neck is a scarf. And Sam's been helping Nana Jo make cookies."

I wince, and she laughs. "Did Penny leave a secret stash before she went on vacation?"

The woman we hired to run the inn because nobody wanted to sell it, but also nobody wants to actually work there anymore, is an excellent cook. And last year she'd taken pity on us and left delicious cookies hidden on the top shelf of the pantry.

"She did." Her cheeks flush. "I ate them all, though."

"Daddy!"

The screen door flies open and I barely have time to brace myself before my arms are full of three-year-old boy. I squeeze Sam and kiss the top of his head, and he's already squirming to be put down.

"I made cookies with Nana Jo!" he tells me, and I'm able to hide the full-body shudder from him. "Come have cookies, Daddy!"

For Sam, I'll eat the cookies and love them, I think. There's nothing I won't do for him. Or for my daughter, who I can't wait to meet.

And the woman who owns my whole heart. Natalie laughs when she opens the screen door and our son takes off running as fast as his little legs will carry him. Then she takes my hand again, stretching to kiss me.

"Merry Christmas, husband. I love you."

I pull her into my arms and bury my face in her hair. "I love you, too. Merry Christmas."

Thank you so much for reading Donovan and Natalie's story! If you enjoyed it, please consider leaving a review on the retailer's site to help other readers discover it.

And turn the page for a complete list of my available books!

Also by Shannon Stacey

To find the most current list of titles visit shannonstacey.com.

Hockey Romances

Here We Go — Book 1

A Second Shot — Book 1.5

The Devlin Group Series

This action-adventure romance series follows the men and women of the Devlin Group, a privately owned rogue agency unhindered by red tape and jurisdiction.

72 Hours — Book 1

On The Edge — Book 2

No Surrender — Book 3

No Place To Hide — Book 4

The Devlin Group Boxed Set: Books 1-4

The Kowalski Series

A contemporary romance series full of family, fun and falling in love.

Exclusively Yours — Book 1

Undeniably Yours — Book 2

Yours To Keep — Book 3

All He Ever Needed — Book 4

All He Ever Desired — Book 5

All He Ever Dreamed — Book 6

Alone With You — Book 6.5

Love A Little Sideways — Book 7

Taken With You — Book 8

Falling For Max — Book 9

What It Takes — Book 10

Feels Like Christmas — Book 10.5

The Sutton's Place Series

Three sisters come together to open the family brewery so their mother doesn't lose everything, but they don't expect to find love along the way. Friends, family, love and laughter!

Her Hometown Man — Book 1

An Unexpected Cowboy — Book 2

Expecting Her Ex's Baby — Book 3

Falling For His Fake Girlfriend — Book 4

The Blackberry Bay Series

Feel good romances about love and laughter in a small town.

More Than Neighbors — Book 1

Their Christmas Baby Contract — Book 2

The Home They Built — Book 3

Cedar Street Novellas

Fun, tropey hijinks in a small town!

One Summer Weekend — Book 1

One Christmas Eve — Book 2

The Boston Fire Series

A contemporary romance series about tough, dedicated (and sexy) firefighters!

Heat Exchange — Book 1

Controlled Burn — Book 2

Fully Ignited — Book 3

Hot Response — Book 4

Under Control — Book 5

Flare Up — Book 6

The Boys of Fall Series

A contemporary romance series about going home again.

Under The Lights — Book 1

Defending Hearts — Book 2

Homecoming — Book 3

Christmas Novellas

Holiday Sparks

Mistletoe & Margaritas

Snowbound With the CEO

Her Holiday Man

In the Spirit

A Fighting Chance

Holiday With A Twist

Hold Her Again

Historical Westerns

Taming Eliza Jane — Book 1

Becoming Miss Becky — Book 2

Also Available

Twice Upon A Road Trip

Forever Again

Heart of the Storm

Slow Summer Kisses

Kiss Me Deadly

About the Author

The *New York Times* and *USA Today* bestselling author of over fifty romances, Shannon Stacey lives in New Hampshire. Her favorite activities are writing romance and really random tweets with her dog curled up at her side, especially during the long winter months. She loves books, coffee, Boston sports, watching way too much TV, and she's never turned down an offering of baked macaroni & cheese.

facebook.com/shannonstacey.authorpage
twitter.com/shannonstacey
instagram.com/shannonstacey

Published by Shannon Stacey

Made in the USA
Columbia, SC
15 December 2024